ANGELES VAMPIRE

BOOK 1

MICHAEL PIERCE

FIONA

"*R*oland Damascus? Never heard of him. You've obviously got the wrong house."

The middle-aged lady answering the door tapped long, red nails against the worn wood, impatient to get back to whatever she'd been doing before I'd so rudely interrupted her. Those nails, nearly talons, quickly grated on my nerves.

She started closing the door, but I stuck out my foot to stop her. "I'm sorry to bother you," I repeated. "But this is 1302 Wheeler, right?"

"That's what it says on the mailbox," she snapped. "Now if you'll excuse me. How about moving your foot? I still have no idea who you're talking about."

The moment I retracted my foot, the door slammed in my face. It wasn't the first time this had happened, and I had a sneaking suspicion it wouldn't be the last. I listened to footsteps marching away on the laminate flooring for a few moments before turning to go.

I'd had a good feeling about this house, but it was now one more address to cross off my list in the endless search for my father. If Mom found out I was still looking for him, she'd probably have an aneurysm. But she didn't understand the need to know where I came from. She knew both her parents—had been raised by them, actually—in a model suburban household. The few pictures I had of my father, on the other hand, were from before I was born, so nearly twenty years earlier. He'd split upon finding out Mom was pregnant with me; I guessed it was a gross understatement, then, to say I hadn't been planned.

I stomped down the steep driveway where my boyfriend, Sean, was waiting by the curb, leaning against the hood of his decade-old red Civic. I was always grateful for him driving me on these wild goose chases I'd regularly map out. Google was such a great resource for most of the world, but a terrible enabler for someone like me.

Colorful chalk drawings decorated the driveway, spilling onto the bisecting sidewalk. The drawing that initially caught my attention was of a three-person family—that I assumed was a mother, father, and daughter—all holding hands. I probably should have turned around from the sight of this drawing alone; it seemed obvious they had their family unit and no space for a troubled outsider like me.

What at first glance I took to be an elaborate sun above the father's head, I soon realized was a compass with a cursive "N" at its zenith, which made me stop and examine it closer.

"I noticed that too. Seems out of place among the clouds and rainbows," Sean said.

"Not when I thought it was a sun," I said, letting the picture go and continuing to the car.

Sean met me by the passenger door and pulled me into a hug. I buried my face in his chest. I knew I wouldn't cry this time, but his warmth was always comforting. Sean didn't say anything, just rubbed his hand across my back while I sighed into his sweater.

"It didn't seem like that went well."

"Not the most pleasant woman, but I've encountered worse," I said, pulling back and offering a weak smile.

Sean nodded with an apologetic expression. "I know," was all he had to say before opening my car door and guiding me in with a gentle nudge.

This neighborhood was only a few cities over from home, which—jumping on the 5 freeway in Orange County Saturday afternoon traffic—meant about a twenty-minute drive. The carpool lane always helped.

Once we were moving, I grabbed my notebook from atop the dashboard and removed the pen from the spiral binding. I flipped to the latest page of notes, and halfway down, crossed out *Gillian Edwards 1302 Wheeler.*

"You up for hitting one more today?" I asked, getting out my phone, ready to type in the address. "It's on the way." Even though I was still frustrated from the previous encounter, I tried to keep my voice light and upbeat. I could still hear those irritating nails against the door.

"Don't you have work soon?" Sean asked as we turned onto the freeway on-ramp.

"In an hour and a half," I said. "Just enough time for one more quick stop."

"See, Fee? You're expecting it to be another dead end." He glanced over at me to gauge my reaction— just in time to see me bite my lip.

"I'm hopeful, but I always go into these things now with zero expectations."

"All the times you've cried on my shoulder doesn't feel like *zero expectations.*"

"That's not fair," I snapped. "Excuse me for having some freakin' emotions. I already told you— you don't have to feel obligated to take me anymore. I can borrow my mom's car once in a while. Alexis can drive me, or I can call an Uber."

"You're missing the point." Sean's attention was solely on the traffic ahead of us now as we careened down the 5 South. "I want to help; I do. It's not that I don't want to drive you, it's that I don't want you to keep doing this to yourself."

I stuffed my phone back in my pocket, knowing the proposed final stop wasn't going to happen. My gaze rested on the name just crossed off my list. "You don't want me to continue pursuing my father just because it's hard? That's a lousy reason to quit pursuing something. Are you just going to quit on us too since I'm a little hard to deal with sometimes?"

Sean was quiet for a moment, his jaw tightening as he considered a response. He'd started driving me on these little excursions even before we officially got together. I opened up with some of my crazy and he seemed to embrace it, which originally brought us closer together. But as the sleuthing hobby became more of an obsession, it began to strain our relationship like obsessions and addictions tend to do. Then the natural progression led to fear of losing him—losing what we'd built over the past fifteen months. I'd already had enough loss for one lifetime.

"I'm not saying to quit because it's hard, I'm saying to quit because it's not worth it," Sean finally said. "I know you've been doing this a long time and I've mostly held my tongue. But what are you hoping to achieve from all this? If you ever do find him, what do you think will happen? What do you think that will really be like? A happy reunion? Maybe not knowing is better than knowing in this instance."

I couldn't accept that. He sounded like Mom,

which irked me. It was always better to know. The worst part was not knowing, not how bad something turned out to be.

"Well?" Sean pressed.

"Well, what? I thought it was rhetorical." I turned my head to stare out the passenger window, not wanting to see his face right now. By a concerned expression alone, he could sometimes coax me over to his side—but not this time. I wouldn't let that happen. This was too important to me. "He's my father," I finally said. "I need to know why. You don't have to understand it. You don't have to agree. But you have to accept it."

We drove a long time in silence, all the way to the off-ramp less than a mile from my apartment. As we sat in silence at a stoplight, and just as the song we'd been listening to transitioned to a commercial, Sean said something sending goosebumps rippling through my body.

"I can't do this anymore," he said, softly.

I finally turned back to him and he glanced my way before the light turned green, then he hit the gas.

"What?" I said, unsure I'd heard right, or trying to convince myself I hadn't. "What does that mean?" I asked, now suddenly sick to my stomach.

Sean took a deep breath. "It means… It means, I can't keep watching you do this to yourself. It's too painful."

"Well, I'm sorry if my family drama's too painful for *you*," I said. "It's no picnic for me, either. Fine. I'll just stop talking about it. You don't have to drive me anymore. I can handle it on my own. Problem solved."

"No." He shook his head. "That doesn't solve anything because you're not going to stop looking for him—no matter what I say—it'll continue to eat you up inside. And I can't be the one to keep picking up the pieces."

"Are you seriously breaking up with me?" Now, I was afraid I might actually throw up. Luckily, we were only a few turns away from my complex. Then I could jump out and vomit in a bush or something. Real classy.

"Fee, I'm so—"

"Don't call me that." I could feel my blood pounding in my ears—right next to the tapping of those devilish nails.

"Fiona..." Sean's attention was now locked on me. "I'm so sorry... I know this is messed up..."

Besides the war raging in my stomach, my eyes were starting to tear up and there didn't seem to be a damn thing I could do about it. I crossed my arms and stared straight ahead—just in time to see an animal darting across the street.

"I just—"

"Sean, watch out!" I screamed.

His head whipped back to the road, his grip

jerking the steering wheel. He swore as we swerved toward another car, then over-corrected in the opposite direction. The front tires of Sean's Civic hit the curb, launching us onto the sidewalk.

A concrete light pole came barreling toward us, which I noticed only a moment before impact. An airbag went off beside me, though nothing deployed on my side. My seat belt didn't lock and it seemed I was flying forward long after the car had stopped, the front end now grotesquely wrapped around the concrete pole. There was no time to react—not even an instant. The last thing I saw was the dashboard as my head slammed straight into it.

2

FIONA

J awoke in a hospital bed with Mom at my side. She'd pulled up a chair and her hand rested on my bandaged arm, being mindful of the IV tube. My head was foggy and I had to squint with the harsh overhead lights. It took a few seconds before images of the crash came flooding back.

"You're okay," Mom said, in the soothing voice she'd used so often when I was a kid. "The doctor says you're going to be fine, though you'll probably have to stay overnight for observations. You banged your head pretty good."

"I—I was wearing my seat belt," I said, groggily. "I don't know what happened."

"I'll get the nurse." Mom lightly patted my arm as she rose.

"How's Sean?"

"I'm fine," I heard a familiar voice say from somewhere in the room behind Mom.

Sean jumped up from a chair against the far wall with a pained smile. One eye looked blackened and a bandage ran across the bridge of his nose, but other than that, he looked unharmed.

"No need, Ms. Winter," he said. "I'll fetch the nurse."

"Thanks, Sean," Mom said as he hurried out of the room, then she returned to her seat by my side. "He's been here nearly as long as I have. He feels terrible."

"He looks good," I said.

"They released him within an hour, but he's already had to start dealing with the police, insurance and all that fun stuff." Mom leaned back in the chair and crossed her legs, her foot bobbing nervously back and forth. "Sean said it was a coyote in the middle of the road."

"I didn't get a good look at it. I thought it was a dog," I said.

"You don't see many coyotes in the middle of the day," Mom replied.

"I haven't seen one near our complex in years," I said, glancing around for the controls to the bed.

Mom realized what I was looking for without me having to say anything. She handed me the remote. "Sean says he thinks he hit the animal," she said.

"I don't remember," I said as the back support of

the mattress lifted until I was nearly in a seated position. "It all happened so fast."

Mom continued. "No animal was found, no blood on the car, or any kind of blood trail leading from the accident."

"What? Are you like some forensics expert now? I saw an animal in the road. We swerved. We crashed into a light pole."

"At least no one else was involved," Mom answered.

Before I could say anything more, a portly young nurse with wide oval glasses strolled into the room. "You're up," she exclaimed. "How're you feeling? How's the pain? Any dizziness or nausea?"

"I'm okay, I guess," I said as she strode up to the monitor. "A little bit of a headache, though."

"That's to be expected. You took a real wallop. Though you're lucky... No fractures. The swelling doesn't seem too bad, but we have an MRI scheduled for you this evening. That will give us a clearer picture of what's going on." The nurse put two fingers to my wrist and stared intently at her watch. Once she sprung back into action, she helped me adjust my pillow for additional back support. "I'll bring you some ibuprofen for the headache and whiplash pain that might not have kicked in yet. Dr. Lagos will come check on you shortly." And as suddenly as she'd arrived, the nurse was gone.

"Well, she was energetic," I said, offering Mom a

smile to help release some of the tension in the room.

"You're not supposed to do this to me, kiddo," Mom said, her bright blue eyes now glistening. "It's you and me against the world, right?"

"Always." She always made me feel guilty when she said stuff like that. But it *was* just us at home; all we had was each other.

The last time I'd been in a hospital bed was when I'd had my appendix out at thirteen. Before then was after the grisly dog attack that left me scarred and my twin sister, Rebecca, dead. We were six. With no father in the picture and the loss of my twin, Mom and I were left with only each other. My grandparents helped when they could, but even they passed a few years later. So, for the better part of a decade, Mom and I were the last of our family name.

The scar running down the right side of my face, from temple to chin, was the result of five surgeries. It had become less noticeable over time, and make-up had certainly helped, but it was something I was always conscious of. And I knew I'd never be as beautiful as my mother because of it, even though I was the spitting image of her in nearly every other way.

I'd seen pictures of her at eighteen that I could have sworn were taken of me. It was almost eerie. She had the same thick chestnut hair, blue eyes, rounded facial features, fair complexion, light freckles, and athletic frame—though she was two inches taller and had to work harder to keep her figure at her age—not that she was old. She was only a few months shy of twenty-one when she'd had Rebecca and me—and was sometimes mistaken for an older sister, rather than my mother. She immensely enjoyed playing into those situations. What middle-aged woman wouldn't?

Thinking about the scar again, I adjusted my hair to cover it even though it was just the two of us in the room.

"Don't hide your face," Mom admonished. "You're such a beautiful girl." She reached over and curled some locks behind my ear.

I smiled shyly, then at the sight of Sean reentering the room, released the hair from behind my right ear.

"My parents are here to take me home," he said, walking over to the bed. "I told them you were awake and looking good. I didn't want to leave without saying goodbye. Let me know if you need anything. I mean it."

"Okay," I said.

"Can I hug you?"

"Of course."

Sean carefully leaned over the bed and I wrapped my arms around him, miraculously without getting the IV tube tangled in our embrace. "We'll talk soon, okay?"

"Okay."

"Bye, Ms. Winter. I'm sorry for—"

"Don't start," Mom said, giving Sean a hug. "I'm just glad you're both okay. Say hi to your parents for me."

"I will," he said, then it was back to just Mom and me—Mom and me against the world.

Dr. Lagos stopped in a short time later and reconfirmed I seemed to be doing well. Mom grabbed herself dinner from the cafeteria and brought me an extra chocolate pudding. She stayed with me during the MRI scan and didn't leave until nearly 10 p.m., by which time I could barely keep my eyes open.

"I can sleep on the couch," she'd offered.

"No, Mom," I'd insisted. "Go home and get a good night's sleep. I'm fine."

"You sure?"

"Positive."

"I'll be back at seven."

"See? I'll hardly even know you're gone."

"Love you, kiddo." She lightly kissed my bandaged forehead, then reluctantly left, but not before giving a slight wave from the doorway.

After another quick check, a new nurse turned off the lights, which didn't do much to darken the room.

The door opened a few minutes later, and I expected it to be the nurse again, perhaps having forgotten something, but it wasn't. Instead, a man in a dark dress shirt and slacks entered.

"Sorry; were you already asleep?" he asked, his voice soft as he remained in the doorway, the hallway light silhouetting him.

"No," I said, trying to figure out if I'd seen him before. His voice didn't sound familiar.

"My name's Matthew Mercer. I'm one of the on-staff counselors for trauma patients. I apologize for the hour. May I come in?"

"Sure," I said, my thumb hovering over the nurse call button on the bed remote. "I didn't realize I needed a therapist."

"You probably don't, but I heard about your accident and wanted to introduce myself and see if I could be of any assistance." Matthew sauntered into the room and carried a chair over from the wall to sit closer to the bed—not close, but close enough.

"You can turn the lights on," I said, pulling the bed covers higher, to keep from feeling exposed in my thin hospital gown.

"It's fine. I don't want to blind you," Matthew said with a chuckle as he took a seat.

Now that he was closer, he seemed younger then I'd expected when he was standing in the doorway—younger than a hospital counselor was supposed to look, given the dozen or so years of extra schooling required. But what did I know? Even though the room was dim, I could still make out he had boyish features. He was tall with a sturdy build, his dark hair combed to one side. The professional clothes he wore looked tailored to fit him perfectly and helped downplay the youthfulness and innocence of his face.

"My files say your name's Fiona Winter. I don't want to assume anything." Matthew produced a smile that lit up the room more than the full lights had done.

My stomach fluttered just from his presence, something I hadn't felt in quite some time. My hand left the vicinity of the call button, and I ran a hand through my hair to make sure it was framing my face. I licked my lips; they were chapped and sore.

"That's correct," I said, finding it suddenly difficult to breathe. "What did you want to talk about?"

"Whatever's on your mind," he said, not allowing that smile to dim. "I'm all ears."

I had so many things on my mind, but none that I particularly wanted to discuss with this beautiful stranger. He was here because of the accident, though—and *I* was here because of it too—so that seemed like a safe and logical place to start.

"Well, it was my first car accident," I said, not knowing exactly how to begin.

"Your boyfriend Sean was driving, right?"

"How did you—"

"It's in the report," Matthew interjected.

"Oh… right. Yes, I guess that's accurate."

"You don't sound so sure about that." Matthew folded his arms across his chest. "Were you actually the one driving? Was he trying to protect you in some way?"

"No; it's not that," I said. "He was driving. It's just… well, we kinda broke up just before the crash."

"And this distracted him from his obligations to the road?" he asked.

"Yes. No. I don't know… This dog—I mean, coyote—came out of nowhere, right in the middle of the road."

"In the middle of the afternoon?"

"Yeah; I know it's weird, but that's what it was," I said. I hated that I didn't remember it more clearly. I still saw a dog, but then again, I always saw dogs. "Then he swerved to get out of the way and hit a light pole."

"Did the car hit the coyote?" Matthew asked.

"Sean said it did," I answered, though still couldn't picture it. "I can't be sure. It's all a blur."

"How are you feeling now?"

"Fine, I guess. I'm told it could have been a lot worse, and I should count myself lucky."

"We should always count ourselves lucky after a brush with death," Matthew said. "You obviously won the point. Would you like to talk about what led to the breakup?"

"Not really," I said matter-of-factly.

"That's fair, considering the late hour and how

we only just met." Matthew stood up and flattened out the front of his slacks. "I should let you get some rest. Thank you for talking with me. It was a pleasure to officially meet you, Fiona Winter." He handed me a business card from his breast pocket. "In case you'd like to talk more."

"Thank you," I said, glancing at the card.

Matthew Mercer, M.D., Executive Director of Operations, Sisters of Mercy Psychiatric Hospital.

"Your search is over," he said.

When I looked up, about to ask him what he meant by that cryptic statement, he was already turning into the hallway, the door steadily swinging closed behind him.

3

FIONA

I'd determined that hospital beds were not at all comfortable. It felt good to be home and Mom had taken the day off work to spend it with me. We passed most of it sprawled on the couch, binge watching old television shows on Netflix. There wasn't much food in the apartment, so we scrounged for lunch and Mom had burgers delivered for dinner. That day reminded me of elementary school and junior high sick days, when Mom had to take off work to stay home with me. We didn't have many of those days anymore. I obviously no longer required a babysitter and things were busier now; I was in my last semester of high school, currently waiting for my college acceptance letters, so I could finalize plans for the next year. Unless I got some pretty big scholarships, I'd be attending a local university. Mom worked several jobs, the combination of which led to some ungodly hours. I spent a good portion of my evenings working at an independent coffee shop down the street called Hot Coffee. I got tips, had flexible hours, and loved all the free drinks. Oh, and I got to work with my two best friends, Alexis and Candace.

"Are you up for one more?" I asked, remote in hand, as the season two episode of *Friends* ended.

"I can't. Damn the labor gods," Mom said, emphatically. She peeled the blanket off herself and adjusted the drawstring knot on her pajama pants. "I need to get up early tomorrow—I already switched shifts once."

"I'm sorry," I said. "You didn't have to stay home with me all day if it was gonna be a problem."

"Nonsense," she said with a smile and kicked down the couch footrest. "I needed some much overdue quality time with my little girl—who isn't quite so little anymore."

"How dare you!" I exclaimed, feigning offense. "I haven't touched a single Oreo all day."

"You know what I mean." She kissed me on top of the head, retreated to her room, and closed the door.

I didn't want to watch another episode alone, so I retreated to my room as well, but not before retrieving the carton of Oreos. Sitting at the foot of the bed, I opened the carton and removed a cookie. I carefully twisted the two sides, having become somewhat of an expert over the years. They almost never broke anymore. I thought of Rebecca again; I always did when the Oreos came out. Rebecca and I had always loved Oreos. She loved the side without the filling and I liked the side with it. We'd complemented each other perfectly. Even after all these years, I still couldn't eat an Oreo whole. And I couldn't eat the side without the filling at all; it just didn't seem right. I popped the filling side of the Oreo into my mouth, placed the naked side on the comforter beside the carton, and grabbed another one.

This always got Rebecca's attention—she was still around.

"Where were you last night, Fee?" I heard her say.

"In the hospital, Becks," I said before popping the second Oreo into my mouth. They'd done their job, but I still craved a few more. I could sometimes consume a whole row in one sitting—even though in my defense, it really wasn't that much since I never ate a complete cookie. I knew it would all catch up with me one day, however.

"Oh my gosh. What happened?"

I'd never been able to see Becca, but I'd begun hearing the voice of my six-year-old twin sister shortly after she died. I was so young when it all started that I didn't even know it was weird, or unnatural, or that I should have been terrified. To me, it was always comforting to hear my sister's sweet tone. Due to the traumatic nature of her death, it seemed her spirit had gotten caught here, trapped somewhere between planes, not allowing her to fully cross over. At least that was the explanation in the movie *Poltergeist*. I didn't know how accurate that was because this kind of thing wasn't supposed to be possible—not in the real world.

I knew she talked to Mom too since Rebecca told me about their conversations, but I never mentioned it to Mom. Somehow, it felt too personal to share. So, I had my six-year-old guardian angel within the walls of my apartment, just another reason why I didn't want to go away to college. I couldn't leave her; we'd shared a room when she was alive, and we still did.

I closed the carton of Oreos and lay back on my bed, telling her all about my ordeal. I kept my voice low to keep from waking Mom, but she slept with a fan on for white noise, so I was never worried about a quiet conversation.

"I want to see under your Band-Aid," she said.

"Fine," I said, knowing she wouldn't stop asking until she got her way. "I don't know what it will look like." I went over to the mirror and began unwrapping the dressing. I cringed as I peeled off the gauze pad underneath; the skin on my forehead was nearly purple, a large bump right in the center of the discoloration. I grabbed a tissue to dab at the skin, still greasy from residual ointment.

"Does it hurt?" Rebecca asked.

"Yeah," I said, collecting all the first-aid items and tossing them in the trash. "But I've got medicine."

"In the morning, you'll feel even better."

"I'm sure I will, though it probably won't look much better." I didn't know how makeup was going to conceal this, but I'd worry about that tomorrow.

I flipped open one of the cards she'd made for me, now taped to my mirror. This one was a Valentine's Day card from when we were five. Then my attention moved to the walls covered in photographs taken by Sean. I especially loved a black and white one he'd taken of me at the beach, minutes before sunset. I was seated in the sand in a long sundress, my hair whipping across my face from the wind. My gaze traveled from one photo to another like connecting the dots to a larger picture.

"I know you liked Sean, but he probably won't be coming around anymore," I said.

"Why, Fee?"

"We broke up yesterday. It's complicated."

"I miss him already," she said.

"I know."

"Why don't you say sorry?" she asked.

"It doesn't really work like that," I said, pulling one of the pictures off the wall, then letting it float to the floor.

"I like that one," she said.

"Me too. But that way, I can't look at it anymore."

I tore another picture off the wall, this one of our reflections in a pool.

"I like that one too."

"Sorry, Becks. I just can't." I felt tears prickling at the edges of my eyes as everything I'd been through in the last twenty-four hours came at me like a flood. The next thing I knew, I was stripping the walls bare, with both hands, until much of the floor was carpeted with fallen pictures.

"Are you gonna throw away the letters too?"

I opened the top drawer of my dresser and removed a stack of *Return to Sender* letters from under my socks. Each of these addresses had already been crossed off my ever-growing list. I dropped onto my bed, wiped my eyes, and flipped through the stack.

"I should," I said.

"Please don't," Rebecca pleaded. "I want them."

"Okay," I said, turning off the light, then crawling under the covers. I hugged the stack of letters like a security blanket and gazed up at my ceiling fan, its whirling blades hypnotic. "Night night, Becks."

"Night night, Fee. Sweet dreams. See you in the morning, in the morning."

"Morning, in the morning," I said and closed my eyes, not expecting the morning to bring much comfort.

4

FIONA

*J*got most of my night shifts covered for the week but returned to work on Friday after school. I usually made it about a half-hour early, giving me time to get my habitual white mocha and sit with Alexis or Candace before our shifts. On quite a few nights, we all got to work together.

"My, how I've missed you," I said, taking a sip of my three-pump, extra hot, extra whipped cream, white mocha.

"I'd be flattered if I thought you were actually talking to me," Alexis said, sarcastically. She strictly drank sweetened black iced teas.

We were sitting at an outside table with the caffeinated drinks we needed to get through the night shift. Candace was already working since she got off school at lunchtime.

"Have you talked to Sean?" Alexis asked, leaning her metal chair back against the storefront glass.

Behind the glass was the coffee roaster, now on display like an antique—merely for show. Hot Coffee was the last coffee shop in the county to roast its own beans, but even we couldn't sustain the practice with all the competition. Now, we were just like every other Starbucks on the block, and I missed the smell of roasting coffee on Sunday mornings. It had brought in people from all over the shopping center, by its aroma alone.

"Do you count texts?" I asked, taking another sip from my porcelain mug, then licking whipped cream off my upper lip. Sean didn't go to our high school, so I usually didn't have a problem with chance meetings.

"Uh, yeah," she said emphatically.

"Then yes, but not much. Just checking up to see how I was doing."

"No mention of the break-up?"

I shook my head, unsure if I was relieved or sad he hadn't brought it up. I surely wasn't going to.

"You need to get out. You've been cooped up at home all week," Alexis said, then slurped the last of her iced tea. She removed the lid and began chomping on the ice.

"Yeah; my mom wants me to get extra rest. And my back's been killing me, worse than my head."

"It already looks way better than earlier in the week."

My phone buzzed in my pocket, so I fished it out and glanced at the screen. It was Candace. I looked up and saw her staring at us from behind the bar. "We've got two minutes!" I shouted.

Alexis turned around to look in through the glass. "What does she want?"

"To take her lunch. She's *starving*," I said, making a big display of fake crying, wanting to make sure Candace could see me.

I was mostly finished with my drink too, so Alexis and I collected our trash and pulled the straps of our black aprons over our heads. The orange words *Caution: Hot Coffee* were emblazoned across the fronts of the aprons. Mine was a little wrinkled from being stuffed in my backpack while Alexis's was crisp and clean, taken from the back seat of her car.

As soon as we clocked in, Candace went on her break, walking over to one of the many eateries surrounding the shop. More often than not, she went with Mexican food, bringing it back here and eating at the bar, so we could still talk in between customers.

Eli was the closing supervisor, with whom I worked with most nights. He was a few years older than the rest of us, working his way through college and trying to get his band discovered. Now that Alexis and I had clocked in, he disappeared into the office to do admin work or call his sorority girlfriend or something. We didn't care because he mostly left us alone.

Alexis took the register and I worked the bar. Alexis loved talking to everyone and I liked to strictly chat with select people. Making the drinks allowed me to be discerning with my conversations. Then there was always Candace to talk to while she ate and waited for her break to be over. Our night rush would start after all the restaurants finished with their dinner rushes.

It felt good to be back at work; it got me out of my head for a while. I was so sick of thinking about Sean, my father, and the accident. I'd been taking ibuprofen all week, which did a good job of numbing the pain throughout my body, but nothing at all in terms of quieting my thoughts.

However, a few hours into my shift, I placed a cappuccino on the bar and called out the name, only to find Sean standing a few feet away.

The mere sight of him made me angry. "What are you doing here?" I asked, ready to start the next drink in the queue—only to realize I'd caught up and there was nothing left to make.

"I wanted to see how you were doing," he said. "You haven't been at work all week."

"You've been checking up on me?" I sounded

offended, even though I really wasn't. If anything, I was slightly flattered.

"Well, yeah… I want to make sure you're doing okay."

"As you can see, I'm totally fine," I said, grabbing a towel and wiping down the espresso wands.

"I can see that," he said, leaning his forearms on the bar. "I was just concerned; that's all."

"My well-being is no longer your concern. You broke up with me, remember?"

"Give me a break," he sighed. "Fee—Fiona, I still care about you. A lot."

"You okay, Fee?" Candace asked, walking up behind me.

I glanced at her and nodded, noticing her giving Sean the death stare.

"Do you want something to drink?" I asked him, then added, "To go?"

"No; I'm good," Sean said, running a hand through his wavy hair. "I'm just glad you're doing well and hope we can find a way to still be friends."

He said goodbye to Alexis as he rounded the counter. They'd been friends first and had introduced us several years earlier. We'd been friends a long time before he finally kissed me.

"Can you believe that guy?" Candace asked, once Sean was gone.

"I dunno. Thought it was sweet," Alexis said from her station by the register.

I was somewhere in the middle. I liked the fact that he was concerned about me, but didn't want to see him right now—not after what had happened before the accident—especially at my place of work. "I think he just had to get it out of his system," I said as another cup was passed to me via Candace.

"Why is it every time I come in here, you girls are just standing around talking?" said a voice from the lobby.

I cringed every time I heard the shrill voice of Mallory Fiennes, the owner's devil of a daughter. She was also a senior, and I had the unfortunate luck of sharing two classes with her.

"I don't know. Maybe you continually show up at just the right time," Candace said, making no move to be productive.

"I don't know why my father doesn't just fire the lot of you."

"Maybe because he likes cute young girls working for him."

Alexis tried to stifle a snicker. I went back to wiping down the counter, not needing any more drama; the quicker we got whatever she wanted, the quicker she'd leave.

Mallory's face scrunched up like a pug and turned bright red at Candace's snide comment. "Well, there's plenty of those to go around, so don't count yourselves special," Mallory finally fired back.

"Hey, Mallory," Eli said, sauntering in from the back room.

Mallory's anger instantly melted away. "Hi, Eli. Can you make me my usual chai?"

"Of course," he said, going over to the espresso bar and edging me out of the way.

Mallory wouldn't let any of us even touch her drinks; only a select few baristas were allowed to craft her chai latte, even though we all knew exactly how she liked it. She was probably afraid we'd spit in it or something. Candace had done worse once when no one was looking. I couldn't do that to a paying customer—though Mallory *wasn't* a paying customer. She simply ran up a tab that never got paid.

Eli slid the finished drink over to her and walked away. Mallory removed the wad of gum she'd been chewing and took a careful sip. "See, ladies, that's how it's done," she said, leaning over the bar, then tossing her gum toward the trashcan behind the counter. It landed on the floor, a few inches from Candace's foot. "Oops... my bad," she said with a malicious smirk.

"If that had hit me—" Candace started.

"You would have done nothing. You've got customers. Chop, chop," Mallory said, turned with her drink, and walked out the door.

"Can I help you?" Alexis said at the register.

"One day…" Candace said. "I'm gonna throw a chai in her smug plastic face."

"I'd like to see that," I laughed, leaned down, and picked up the gum with a piece of wax paper.

"Eli, we need help out here!" Alexis yelled.

"And I'm off!" Candace called, removing her apron.

THE NEXT FEW hours flew by due to the steady stream of people coming in. I barely thought of Sean or Mallory during that time. It wasn't until things died down and we had nothing left to do but clean, that my thoughts began to wander. Alexis bugged me about hanging out after our shift since I hadn't gotten out in over a week. She could tell I was distracted and insisted I needed a little R&R.

"Fee, are you even listening to me?" Alexis asked, putting up the chairs in the lobby.

I had the espresso machine in pieces, giving it a good deep clean. Eli was in the office counting the tills—or talking to his girlfriend or anything to get out of having to clean with the rest of us.

"Of course," I said, absently.

"Then did your mom say yes?"

"Say yes about what?"

"You said you were listening!" she whined. "About getting out tonight."

"Yeah; sorry," I replied. "I called her. She wasn't keen on the idea, but finally caved."

"Perfect!" she exclaimed. "Candace will be back by the time we're done."

"It's a party," I said sardonically and continued scrubbing the espresso machine.

5

FIONA

e drove out into the foothills, past the toll road, and seemed to leave civilization behind. Candace led the way in her older sister's green Mustang. I rode with Alexis in her beat-up Chevy pickup. The poor thing still had a tape deck and manual crank windows. And it definitely possessed no airbags, which never used to bother me. It made me a little nervous now.

There was one wooden sign for Black Star Canyon that was barely legible, and a few hundred feet later, we turned onto a gravel road wide enough for a single car. The sad excuse for a one-lane road was lined with short wooden posts. On the left, I could see the earth fall away as we worked our way into the canyon. A rock wall grew on the right at a similar rate to the cliff on the other, descending into darkness. There were no street lights out here, only moonlight—and the little sliver hanging in the sky was barely visible. We could only see as far as the headlight beams would allow. And then we came to a gate stretching across the road, forcing us to stop.

Candace was already out of her Mustang and opening the trunk. Alexis and I got out and helped with the supplies Candace had brought—a fire log, pink lighter, the fixings for smores, a six-pack of hard cider, and three folding chairs. Her sister was twenty-two and usually willing to get us alcohol.

Candace left her headlights on while the three of us hopped over the gate with our supplies and settled in an open spot in the gravel. The driveway extended deep into the canyon, disappearing into the darkness beyond the reach of the headlights.

After kicking around some of the rocks, Candace placed the fire log in the center of the makeshift firepit and set it ablaze.

"Burn, baby, burn!" she yelled into the night, her hands hovering above the undulating flames.

Alexis laughed as she scrolled through her phone, found a song we'd all heard way too often, and turned on her pocket-sized Bluetooth speaker.

Once she was done with her silly witch dance, Candace returned to her sister's Mustang and killed the headlights.

I wouldn't say we did this regularly, but we'd

been to Black Star Canyon after dark a number of times. It was our secret place to escape the outside world—our little haven under the stars.

Something about the canyon always made it about ten degrees cooler than even a mile down the road. The weather was already warming with the promise of spring, but the nights were still cool. However, the fire prevented any need for a jacket.

We spread out around the fire in our beach chairs. Candace passed me one of the pear hard ciders, then offered one to Alexis. I tossed the cap into the flames and took a swig.

"Thank you, Bethany. That hits the spot," I said, speaking of Candace's older sister.

"Thought you could use it after... well, everything," Candace said, balancing her bottle on her knee.

"You're not on medication, are you?" Alexis asked.

"Not since this morning," I said. "I don't hurt that bad."

"You were in a car accident. That's crazy. Sean sent me pics of the car. It was *messed up.*"

I hadn't even seen pictures of the accident.

"That car was made of tinfoil; what do you expect?" Candace said.

As if she was reading my mind, Alexis passed me her phone, open to a picture of Sean's wrecked

Civic, wrapped around the light pole. I flipped through the few pictures she had—of the car, emergency vehicles, a growing crowd of bystanders, and even one of me being taken away on a gurney. I was out cold; no memory of any of this.

"Wow…" I said, giving her back the phone and taking another sip of my cider. "I feel like I'm dead, looking down at my own body."

"Yeah; I can't believe that was you," Alexis said. "But look at you now, good as new."

"I don't know about that." I touched the chilled bottle to the bump on my forehead and winced. "At least it's going down a little."

"It's not even noticeable," Candace said. "You're so self-conscious about your scars. No one even notices."

She'd said that to me countless times before, but I always felt like people were staring. I always saw the jagged scar running down the right side of my face each time I looked in the mirror, smaller lines shooting off the main one like the branches of a tree. If I couldn't help but look at it, I didn't understand how others could resist it, either. Whenever I spotted people's eyes on me, I knew what was catching their attention.

"I know," I said, acknowledging her statement, but not agreeing.

"It's not really over is it?" Alexis asked. "I mean,

you're not Candace and Brian, breaking up like every five minutes."

"Hey," Candace protested. "We've been back together for five months."

"And how many times did you break up before then—or threaten to since?"

"I—I don't keep count of that sort of thing."

"Exactly my point," Alexis said, smugly.

"I think it really is," I said. "I don't know how to get past this one. I can't stop looking for my father. And I'm certainly not going to do it for *him*."

"Nor should you," Candace said. "It was totally unfair of him to ask."

"But I'm sure he's kicking himself," Alexis said. "He knows he screwed up. He'd be stupid to let someone like you go. Give it some time."

"I always thought you could do better," Candace said. "I didn't want to say anything before, but there it is."

"You'll say that about anyone," Alexis said.

"When she gets that little extra confidence, she'll realize it's true."

"How about not talking about me like I'm not even here," I snapped, finishing my cider, and setting the empty bottle next to my chair.

"You can do better than that guy, Fee. You don't deserve to settle," Candace said, looking me square in the eyes.

"I don't know about that," I said.

"I do."

"Sean was not *settling*," Alexis chimed in. "He was just a stupid high school boy, doing what stupid high school boys do—freaking out when things start to get serious."

"Well, we'll be out of that dump soon enough," Candace said, handing me another cider. "A fresh start for college is a good thing."

"What about you and Brian?" Alexis asked. "You planning to break it off for good this summer?"

Candace laughed as she moved onto her second cider as well. "Guess we'll find out soon enough."

Alexis was still nursing her first drink, not even halfway through the bottle—more interested in tearing at the label than drinking the contents.

I was tired of talking and arguing about Sean. I couldn't see us getting back together, so I simply wanted to move on. "You know what would make me feel better?" I asked. Both girls could probably guess, especially once I reached for the bag of smores ingredients.

As I skewered a marshmallow and stuck it into the fire, the music from Alexis's iPhone went quiet. When she checked the phone, it seemed to have suddenly died.

"It was fully charged," she whined, slapping it against her palm like that was the miracle fix-it strategy for electronics.

The only other sound besides Alexis's complaining was the crackling from our fire.

And then I heard it—the crunch, crunch of approaching footsteps on the gravel. They were heavy, pervading the air thickly like the march of army boots, and when the steps drew closer, I was able to distinguish several distinct sets.

Not one of us moved. We sat, frozen to the spot.

Slowly, nervously, I turned to the direction of the incoming footsteps and saw several beastly shadows floating toward us. After a few more moments, the footsteps stopped.

"Hello?" The single audible word came from Candace. Her voice tremored and crackled along with the fire, her phone—now in her hand as a comforting lifeline—also just as dead.

I checked mine as well, but it was as useless as the others, which made no sense at all.

No reply came from the human-sized shadows now standing behind our cars.

After a prolonged silence, the sound of tires on gravel could be heard. They too were inching closer. But I didn't see anything. The phantom car sounded so near now, but still it was shrouded in the darkness. Then, there was a shadow the size of a truck creeping slowly closer.

"We don't want any trouble." It was Candace again, her voice practically squeaking now.

After another elongated moment of silence, I was

blinded by white light. Two xenon globes split the darkness like tiny suns, causing the three of us to shield our eyes with raised hands. There wasn't time for any more reactions. Once the spotlights hit us, everything began to unravel quickly.

6

MATTHEW

I'd been keeping a closer eye on Fiona since her accident the previous weekend and knew we couldn't prolong this any longer. I urged the Assembly we needed to move fast before any more potential *accidents* befell her.

As soon as I found out she'd be returning to work on Friday evening, we scheduled the operation. It was just a bonus that she and her friends decided to drive out into the canyons—nicely isolated—for some girl bonding time.

Trent and I walked up the gravel driveway in the dark. We were dressed in black army fatigues and black ski masks to maintain anonymity and drive up the intimidation factor. The loud voices and laughter from these girls could be heard from at least a half mile away. I could also hear music from one of their cellphones—probably with a Bluetooth speaker. Trent had the Beacon and as soon as we turned the last bend, he'd be ready to press the button. Both of us had been dropped off at the edge of the main road, so the Land Rover wouldn't be within the Beacon's range when it emitted the pulse. All electronics within 250 feet would be knocked out—not completely fried, just reset. The cars would need to be jump-started, but that was just one part of the operation.

"You ready?" Trent asked, his voice muffled slightly from the ski mask.

"Let's get this over with," I said.

Trent hit the button on the small metal device in his hand and everything fell silent ahead of us. Typically, all the lights would have gone out too, but these girls had lit a bonfire. Our footsteps were now quite noticeable, as was the high-pitched whine of the drone overhead—the eye in the sky—which was circling up high enough to where it wasn't affected by the pulse of the Beacon. But that didn't matter anymore. The girls ahead weren't going anywhere.

After a good thirty count, the drone operator back at the base would radio Floyd in the Land Rover that it was safe to proceed. Trent and I waited in the shadows for the cavalry to arrive.

"Hello?" It was the girl with the long black hair—Candace Raine—and her voice wavered as much as her hands.

I pulled out a plastic handgun of True North's

own design from my hip holster. Lightweight, accurate, deadly, and untraceable. It wasn't something I needed, but would certainly get their attention.

The Land Rover was on its way, crunching along the gravel, and when the tires stopped, the night seemed to get even quieter.

"We don't want any trouble." It was Candace who spoke up again. She obviously fancied herself as the hero of the group.

It will be no trouble at all, I thought.

Two seconds later, the headlights from the Land Rover flooded the area with bluish white light, signaling it was time to use that extra intimidating force.

The driver's side door of the Land Rover burst open, and Floyd emerged from the SUV also wearing a ski mask. Then the three of us descended on the frozen and dumbfounded teenagers.

"Everybody stay where you are!" Trent yelled. "Hands up where I can see them!"

"Show me your hands!" I demanded.

The eye in the sky was flying away now, back to base, its small whine quickly growing fainter, then non-existent as it glided over the foothills.

All guns were up and aimed at the shaking teenage group. The other girl—Alexis Andrews— was crying now. Candace looked dazed and helpless, and Fiona's blue eyes couldn't have grown any wider. I almost felt bad doing this to her—but it was what we'd always done, and she couldn't be seen as getting special treatment.

The True North soldiers secured the perimeter and quickly corralled the girls into a neat little group in front of the Mustang.

"Who are you people?" Candace asked, meekly.

"That's not for you to know," I growled and grabbed Fiona's trembling arm, dragging her away from her friends.

"What do you want with her?" Candace asked.

Alexis was simply a blubbering mess of sobbing and pleading, most of which wasn't coherent enough to understand.

Trent spoke up. "The real question you should be concerned with is what are we going to do with *you?*"

"Please just take our wallets and cars. Just let us go. Don't hurt us," Alexis finally managed to say.

"We don't want anything from you," Floyd said. He grabbed Alexis, then Trent snatched Candace.

"No, no, no—what are you doing?" Candace screamed when she saw the first syringe.

"Don't worry. You'll just feel a small prick," Trent said and snorted with laughter. He loved that line.

Candace's screams ceased a moment later, Alexis's shortly after that.

"What are you doing to my friends?" Fiona cried.

I loosened up on her arm. She was no longer

fighting to get away, knowing there was nowhere to run and no one left to help her.

"They'll be fine," I said, forgetting the terror act for a moment and speaking gently. "The serum will knock them out for approximately six hours. The worst part will be the hangover when they wake up. These last fifteen to twenty minutes will be a complete blur, a common side effect of grossly over-drinking. You're the only one who'll remember we were ever here."

"Who *are* you?"

"Someone sent to collect you," I said.

Floyd and Trent were now sliding the limp bodies of the girls into the back seats of their cars. Then Trent hopped the gate to put out the small bonfire.

"Everything good?" I called out.

"All secure," Floyd said.

"Then you know what to do."

"Sure do."

"That's our cue to leave, sweetheart," I said and walked Fiona to the Land Rover.

"Why are you doing this?" Fiona cried, tears now streaming down her face. "Please, just let me—let us go home. We'll forget this ever happened."

I swung open the back door and pushed Fiona in. She fought at first, but when she saw the final syringe in my hand—the special one intended specifically for her—she quickly deflated, knowing her time was up and there was nothing she could do about it.

These types of things had never bothered me before. Many of our operations were designed and put into practice because of me, but what we were doing suddenly began to feel... barbaric. But it was as it had always been. You can't change the past and you can't change the future. This was just how things had to be.

"I know you're scared and I know this is disorienting, but I need you to listen to me carefully. You are not going to be harmed tonight, and neither are your friends. Before we go, I am extending you an exclusive invitation—one that doesn't need acceptance quite yet. You'll understand more soon enough."

"Where are we going?" Fiona sniffled between each drawn-out word.

"North," I said before sticking her with the syringe.

7

FIONA

othing could have prepared me for what I saw when I awoke. It simply didn't make sense. My new surroundings felt more surreal than any dream I could remember.

I was in a round room constructed entirely of glass—walls, floor, ceiling. This was then connected to what looked like a giant machine by a glass tube that bisected the space, continuing all the way to the floor. It was like I was in a glass cylinder, one hundred feet wide, suspended in midair. But as strange as the room was, it was what lay beyond the glass that really took my breath away.

The expanse of black open space seemed endless. Millions of stars brighter than I had ever seen before, surrounded me on all sides. The full moon shone like a brilliant sphere many times larger than it should have been—like it was right here and I could almost reach out and touch it. Then below me, through the floor, I saw a vision only previously seen in pictures or movie screens—the giant blue and green marble of Earth. White clouds swirled over its surface and I could make out the outline of North America.

What the hell am I looking at?

I couldn't believe anything I was seeing. I'd been kidnapped from Black Star Canyon, drugged, and had woken up in outer space. I supposed the machine above me was some kind of spaceship or station. There was no way this could be real. Unless…

How long was I out?

I looked myself over and confirmed I was still in the same clothes I remembered wearing when taken. My pockets were empty—my phone, gone.

I was on all fours now, arms and legs shaking as I felt suspended in space, my hands and knees pressed against the thin glass separating me from the rest of the universe. I couldn't even appreciate the beauty outside because of rising nausea in the back of my throat.

"What's going on?" a voice asked.

That's when I noticed I wasn't alone. I had to count them several times to make sure I wasn't imagining them. Three others—three other people were waking up on the glass floor, just as I had.

"You know just as much as I do," a man said. He

looked to be somewhere in his mid-twenties, but already balding. He wore silver-rimmed glasses and unflattering khakis.

"I know nothing," the dark-skinned woman said. She also looked like she was in her twenties, possibly approaching thirty. She was super petite with defined wiry muscles and thick black hair no more than a few inches long.

"Then we're even," the guy said.

"Where are we?"

When I heard the third voice, I thought my ears were playing tricks on me. However, my eyes were just as treasonous as I realized the voice belonged to Mallory Fiennes. She'd been wearing capris and a scoop-neck top when I'd seen her last, but was now in a flowery sundress. I knew she could have gone home to change after visiting the coffee shop, but her change of clothes was still disorienting.

"Fiona?" Mallory asked suspiciously.

"You two know each other?" the guy asked.

"Mallory, what's going on?" I asked.

"Somebody better start explaining something," the other woman insisted, getting to her feet. She had a hard time finding her balance, like the floor was uneven.

But before anything more could be said, a low humming sound came from the glass tube in the center of the room. Lights somehow built within the glass illuminated the general enclosure. A group of cloaked figures slowly descended from inside the tube—which appeared to be a glass elevator with a glass floor, making it look like they were floating.

Nearly transparent doors in the tube opened and seven cloaked figures in an odd assortment of masks stepped into the glass room. All seven of the cloaks contained hoods that were also up, and the combinations of hoods and masks hid their entire heads. Each of the figures wore black gloves, so there wasn't a single inch of visible skin. Behind the cloaked figures appeared a man I had seen before— from the hospital—Matthew something. He had given me a business card for a psychiatric hospital, along with a cryptic message.

Your search is over. I was more afraid than ever to contemplate what that meant.

The seven cloaked figures walked further into the room and examined us quietly. Matthew remained inconspicuously behind them.

A cloaked figure with a mask sporting a long, crooked beak-nose stepped forward and addressed us.

"I speak for everyone here today when I say welcome." The voice was that of a woman. "I know you're scared and confused and want to know what you're doing here. The fact is, you are here because you have been chosen. Though you may not believe it now, your invitation should be considered a great honor. There are very few people in this world who will have the opportunity that you have right now if you choose to accept this invitation, and not many will learn the truth until it is too late.

"The True North Society does not exist. It is a myth, an urban legend, just another story that's been told for decades. Or so we would have you believe. The True North Society is nowhere and yet it is everywhere. As far as you know it is still a myth, yet you are here this evening before us. I will neither confirm nor deny our existence to you here tonight. With all that you have heard and what you have now seen, you must ask yourselves—what do I believe?

"I am not here to convince you one way or another. I am here to offer you an opportunity to learn the truth. But the truth will not come easily. To be granted access to learn the secrets we defend with our very lives each and every day, you will have to complete rigorous training and prove yourselves worthy. This training will be the hardest thing you've ever had to do. It will test your loyalty, honor, strength, and sense of sacrifice to see if you have what it takes to defend the secrets." The cloaked woman stopped and took a breath. She glanced back at the accompanying cloaked figures behind her, who all nodded in unanimous approval.

Every moment of this experience was growing stranger and stranger. We were in a transparent room overlooking the cosmos before a clan of grownups in Halloween costumes, giving us the "opportunity of a lifetime" speech. It was all too much. *What do I believe?* I had no idea. Sure, I had heard of the True North Society before, but I equated them to the Illuminati. I'd seen their compass symbol randomly on the internet, but it didn't mean anything to me. I didn't know if they were real or not and never did any research on them —conspiracy theories had never interested me. How had my search led me here?

"Why should we believe anything you're saying?" the woman asked. She was the first to speak up.

"Because you can look out these windows and know there is something very special about this place, and as an extension, something very special about us and what we have to offer," the speaker said. "You will have the choice whether to accept or to go back to your ordinary lives. The choice is yours and the opportunity is yours. I am not here to tell you how to live your lives. You have seen something this night that very few people in the world have ever seen, or will ever see, and may choose what you will do with this newfound knowledge. Are you the type of person that lets an opportunity slip through your fingers? Or are you someone who can recognize a great opportunity for what it is and seize it?" She dramatically held out her arm and clenched a gloved fist.

"I think of myself as a pretty proactive woman," the female captive said. "But all this—well, I don't know what all this is. You're not convincing me of some great opportunity I'm missing out on. Kidnapping me in the night does not earn my trust. How can you convince me any of this is real? I see this more as an elaborate soundstage. Is that what this is? Are we in some hanger in the middle of the desert?"

The speaker shook her head. "If you can't see the opportunity, then you will never see the truth," she said and stepped back in line with the other cloaked figures.

"Why were we chosen?" I asked, and I cringed at the sound of my own soft, mousy voice.

"Each of you was chosen for a specific reason, by a specific person," one of the other cloaked figures said, this one bearing the deep voice of a middle-aged man. "Each of you is special, which is the first thing you must know."

"Who chose me?" I asked.

"And me?" the woman repeated.

Mallory and the man were both oddly quiet—almost like they knew something.

"If you choose to accept your candidacy, then you shall find out," the original female speaker said. "If not, then your question will remain unanswered and all of this will become a distant memory, like trying to hold onto a fleeting dream after being woken prematurely."

I was chosen... By whom? All I could think of was my father...

"I understand this is frustrating," she continued, as if reading my mind. "But this is the way it has to be if we want to protect ourselves. We must be extremely cautious with whom we let into our inner circle. We have remained a myth since 1949 and will keep up that guise until the end of days. Every group must take precautions. Now think of the precautions it takes to defend a group that claims not to exist.

"I understand this is a big decision and I urge that you not take it lightly. And that is why we will not be asking for your acceptance or abnegation here this evening. You will have exactly one week to reflect and decide."

One of the other masked men stepped forward and pulled small black cards from beneath his robe. They looked like thick business cards. He approached me first and handed me one.

Once he moved on, I examined the card, which contained nothing more than a phone number. I flipped it over, only to find the other side blank.

"Take the next week to reflect on what you have seen and heard today, and if you want to know more —if you desire to know the truth—then call the number on the card and your candidacy will begin," the original speaker said. "Show it to no one. Tell no one what you have seen here tonight. Once you've made the call, instructions will be provided. If you do not call within the week, then consider your opportunity gone."

Once the four of us had our cards, and the cloaked figure was back in line with the others, the primary speaker continued. "I speak for my fellow members as well as myself when I say thank you for your time tonight. I apologize for the dramatics, but they are integral to the mystery of our identity as an organization. I do hope for your full consideration and potential acceptance within one week's time. My name is Janice Bolt, the president of the True North Society and the United World Coalition. I look forward to welcoming each of you to the Society and shaking your hands. You may not have known that you were searching for your True North, but you were—and you've found it." And with that, the cloaked figures stepped back into the glass elevator and ascended into the station above.

The only person left with us was Matthew. I could see him more clearly now than when he visited me in the hospital. He had steely gray eyes and fair skin. Even in the light, he looked as youthful as before, not much older than I was. But there was a hardness to his eyes that suggested more experience than his appearance suggested. Matthew was not in formal clothes like in the hospital, but black military-style fatigues—like the men who had attacked my friends and me in the canyon.

"Was it you?" I asked, my fear turning to anger.

"Me who took you?" Matthew asked.

"Yeah," the lady said accusatorily. "You're dressed like the men who snatched me too."

"I can't be everywhere at once," Matthew said, suppressing a slight grin.

"Is this funny to you?"

"My job has its moments. Now, I'm going to be putting each of you under again, then you'll be brought home."

"What if I'm ready to say yes now," the man said.

"You'll still need to call the number," Matthew answered. "Protocol."

The man looked severely disappointed, but didn't put up a fight. Matthew decided to start with him, sticking a syringe into his neck, then gently guiding him to the floor.

Mallory was also oddly quiet and went next without an argument, though she gave me a vicious glare before her eyelids shut and she lost consciousness as well.

"I am so calling in sick tomorrow," the lady said as Matthew approached her. "I need a drink."

"A drink is always tempting," Matthew said with a chuckle. "Hold still. I don't want this to hurt."

A few seconds later, the woman was out, and Matthew lay her body on the glass floor.

"Your turn," Matthew said, now standing before me with one more syringe in his hand.

"Is this what you meant by my search being over?"

He nodded, his expression looking conflicted—
or pained in some way. I felt myself shaking again.

"What do you know about my search?"

"I know a great deal about you, Fiona Winter," Matthew said.

Gooseflesh prickled throughout my body from the combination of his intense gaze and unsettling words. "You're not a trauma counselor," I said, stating a fact.

"No."

"Then who are you?"

"Make the call and you'll find out," he said, bringing an empty hand to my neck.

I wanted to flinch, but was suddenly frozen in place, even when he tucked my bangs behind my ear and exposed the long scar running down my cheek. He tenderly brushed his thumb over the scar—something I never allowed anyone to do—but couldn't move. Then he raised the needle to the opposite side of my neck and injected me with the clear serum. Matthew's face faded from view as I felt myself falling. Everything went black.

8

FIONA

I was so relieved to awake in my own bed and still be in my clothes from the night before. The only things taken off were my shoes, which were set neatly on the floor by my nightstand. My purse that had been left in Alexis's car peeked out from around the nightstand's corner.

I felt groggy, but not overly sick. Sitting up, my head began to spin, coaxing me to return down to the pillow.

The sun was up behind the curtains, the same sight that lit up my room most mornings. My door was closed, and the ceiling fan blew steadily overhead, its soft hum lulling me to sleep at night. Quickly surveying my room from the bed, everything appeared in order.

I thought back to the events of the night before, which now merely felt like a vivid dream. It was hard enough to process the information, not to mention what I'd seen inside that glass room. Then there was the strange presence of the man from the hospital.

Matthew.

And Mallory. I couldn't imagine how we were related in this messed up situation. While my mind reeled, grasping for any theories or potential answers, I remembered the card given to me by the cloaked figure. Immediately, I searched my pockets and found the black card with the white phone number.

It's real... Last night was real...

My hand shook as I gazed upon the number. It was physical evidence that last night really happened —that it hadn't been some crazy dream. At least something about it was real. Maybe I'd been injected with a hallucinogen, transporting me into outer space and summoning the monsters in black robes. It was less farfetched than what appeared to be happening.

I sat up again, and this time my head was more cooperative. The clock on my nightstand read 10:30, which was sleeping in super late for me. I was almost surprised Mom hadn't come in to check on me. Well, maybe she had.

I bent over the edge of the bed, first noticing my phone charging on the floor. I grabbed my purse and thanked God my wallet was still in there; it still contained my ID, cards, and money. Though, unfortunately, no one had slipped in any extra bills.

Once I was convinced none of my things had been stolen, I turned my attention to my phone. Three missed calls and four messages. I was so relieved to discover Alexis and Candace had both tried to contact me this morning. Not only were they alive, but they seemed concerned for my well-being, which meant they were okay.

I called Alexis first, and she picked up on the second ring like the phone was in her hand, desperately waiting for a call.

"Fee, I thought you were dead in a ditch somewhere," Alexis said, her voice panic-stricken. "You didn't wake up in a ditch, did you?"

"No," I said. "I woke up in my bed. What the hell happened last night?" I needed to know what she recalled before offering any information of my own.

"I was hoping you could enlighten me—us; I already talked to Candace," Alexis said. "Neither of us remembers much of anything. The three of us are sitting around the fire talking, the next thing I know I'm waking up in my bed this morning. I have no memory of leaving the canyon, driving you home, driving myself at all... Nothing. How're you? Do you remember anything?"

"The ciders must have been harder than we thought," I laughed, but immediately realized how insensitive that was.

"It's not funny," Alexis snapped. "I don't remember having more than one cider. I wasn't even buzzed."

"How are you feeling this morning?" I asked.

"Like death. I've already thrown up twice. Please tell me you remember something. I've already had to tell my parents I've got food poisoning because I can't tell them I was drinking and driving."

"I dunno," I said. "I don't really have any new information to share. I haven't thrown up, but my stomach's pretty messed up too. I don't remember you driving me home, but somehow made it, safe and sound. How's Candace doing?"

"What do you think? She's freakin' shaken up too. I don't get it. I've been drunk before, but never had a total blackout."

I couldn't believe it; their minds really had been wiped of the unexpected events of last night. It seemed they didn't have any recollection of the attack and my absence for God knew how long. But it did seem to happen all in the span of one night, which made me that much more curious. I gazed at the mysterious card as Alexis freaked out about going to jail and ruining her life. At least they hadn't damaged her car to make the drunk driving cover story more believable.

"I assume no one saw you come in last night?" I asked.

"If they had, no one's mentioning anything. And

it's not like I can openly ask them a question like that," Alexis scoffed.

"Yeah; I haven't even faced my mom yet," I said. "But she may have had an early shift this morning. I can't keep track of her ever-changing work schedule."

"You guys should put each other's work schedules in your calendars."

"Give me a break; that would be too organized," I said with a laugh. "Well, I'm just glad you're okay— that we all are."

"I say we never speak of this again."

"Speak of what? What we can't remember? Brilliant plan."

"It's just freaking me out and I—I—I'm gonna be sick again!" Alexis choked out, then the line went dead.

Candace didn't pick up, so I texted to let her know I was still alive. I placed the phone and black card on the nightstand while listening carefully to see if I could hear Mom in the main living area of our apartment. At least for now, everything was quiet. I gazed around my room and my recently cleared walls. Per my promise to Rebecca, I hadn't thrown all of Sean's photos away, but stuck them in the bottom drawer of my desk. Mom hadn't said anything to me about it yet, but I knew she'd have noticed.

Before leaving my room, I quickly changed into

some pajamas, worked my hair into a bun, then opened the door like it was just another normal Saturday morning. I drifted through the living room and over to the kitchen. There was no sign of Mom, but a still warm half pot of coffee remained on the countertop. When would Mom ever learn I wouldn't drink stale coffee? I got all the free coffee I wanted, so brewing a fresh pot wasn't a waste.

I got more coffee going, then wandered into her bedroom as the last place she'd be if she was still home. Her hair straightener was on the counter, the unplugged cord reaching the floor, but it was cold now. I decided she hadn't just left.

I guess I'm safe, I thought, ambling back into the kitchen. I didn't even know how to start processing everything that had happened the night before, so I made a bowl of Cinnamon Toast Crunch, poured myself a coffee with white mocha creamer, and took a seat on the couch in front of the television. I ate and drank and watched a recorded reality show. Mom recorded a bunch of shows because of her erratic work schedule. There was always something to choose from.

Once I was done with my cereal, I took out the carton of Oreos. I pulled one apart and set the naked side on the coffee table, then dunked the side with the frosting in my cinnamon-infused milk. I couldn't just eat one, so I broke apart two more cookies and scarfed them down. At that point, I knew I'd had enough—sugar overload. I gazed down at the stack of three Oreo halves and smiled. With a sudden burst of energy, I threw my dirty dishes in the sink, stashed the cookies in the pantry, then scooped up the Oreo halves. With Mom out of the apartment, it was the perfect time to speak with my dear sister.

"Thanks, Fee," Becca said shortly after I placed the stack of cookie halves on my desk. "They smell so good."

"I'm glad you're around, Becks," I said.

"Who was that man who carried you in last night?"

"You saw me come home?" I was anxious to get some of the blanks filled in.

"He carried you through the window," she said. "It was really late."

"We came in through the window? But my window was locked."

"Nope," she simply said, but I knew it had been. I didn't know how he'd opened it but was confident I was right.

"What happened afterward?" I asked.

"He tucked you in bed. You were sleeping."

"Did he, umm… touch me or anything while I was sleeping?"

"He took off your shoes."

"And that's all?"

"He touched your cheek—the one with the scar."

That made me angry. That was twice now. I

didn't want anyone touching it, let alone some handsome guy I barely knew. I started to blush just thinking about how handsome he was, then scolded myself for it.

"Fee, who was he?" Becca asked.

"I—I don't really know," I answered honestly. "His name is Matthew—Matthew Mercer. Something super weird happened to me last night." I gave her a quick version of my recollection of the events —how I was abducted, ended up on a space station with a bunch of creepy masked people, told it was some great honor to be admitted into the True North Society, then dumped off at home with a card to call them if I wanted to become a candidate.

"I've heard of them before."

"From who?"

"You, I think."

"I've never mentioned them to you before," I said. "They've barely ever been on my radar."

"Maybe Mom then."

"Why would she be talking to you about them?"

"I dunno," Becca said, sounding exasperated. "Maybe she was talking to someone else."

"You're not helping." I fell back on my bed, then glanced at my phone for messages. Candace had responded to my text, ranting that she was going to sue the cider manufacturer. "I don't know what to do." I draped my arm across my eyes. "They said each one of us was special. We were chosen."

"By who?"

"I don't know. They wouldn't tell us, saying we needed to call to find out. Everyone I know is normal—at least relatively so. I mean, Mallory was there too, so I don't know exactly what that means. Could Dad have something to do with this? Maybe after all these years searching for him, he's reaching out to me?"

"You should call," Becca said. "I wish I could go with you."

"But the whole thing was so crazy, Becks. You have no idea. Well, maybe you do because you're dead. I dunno."

"Yeah; it stinks sometimes," she said, forcing a smile onto my lips. "What if it is Dad?"

"Then I can slap him like I've always dreamt of doing."

"Slap him for me too."

"You got it, Becks." I grabbed the black card and looked it over, transfixed on the sequence of numbers. "I'm scared of what I'm getting myself into."

"Don't be scared. I'm with you."

"I know… but you can't come with me. At least I have someone to talk to about it." I took a deep breath, then reached for my phone. "Here goes nothing," I said and dialed the number.

9

MATTHEW

"My name is Matthew, and I'm an alcoholic," I said, and paused as applause rang out in the church activity room. I looked out at the hard and weathered faces of twenty other addiction-stricken individuals, all sizing me up to determine if my problem was worse than theirs. If they only knew what true addiction was. "I've been sober for thirty-two days, and on not one of them did I not think about taking a drink. I know for some of you, it gets easier as the days go by, even though it never really leaves for good—the need. But for me, that need never seems to lessen. It's always there just as powerful, just as seductive. So, every day I must remind myself that today is not the day I will be seduced into taking another sip. I'll tell myself the same thing tomorrow, and repeat it again and again throughout the day. *Today is not the day I will be seduced into taking another sip.*

"I've struggled with this for many years and have fallen off the wagon a number of times. I don't know if this will be the time it finally takes or if I'll be doomed to continue repeating the same process, but I will keep trying. That's all I can do, right? That's all any of us can really do.

"I know I'm new here, but I appreciate you having me. I appreciate your support and allowing me this moment to speak—because it won't be often." I smiled, and a few people around the room laughed, including my sponsor, Jezebel. "That's all I really have to say, so thank you. I guess I'll try some of your fine gourmet coffee in the back. Hopefully, it will help satiate the thirst a wee bit."

I left the front of the room to the sound of more sporadic chuckles and shook a few hands on my way to the refreshments table on the far side of the room.

This was only my second AA meeting with this group, though I had attended many before, jumping around to numerous different groups—never staying in one more than a few years. I'd also been through as many sponsors since I could never comfortably get into the true nature of my addiction.

I grabbed a paper cup and filled it from the carafe labeled *House Blend*. I never added creamer or sugar; it simply didn't matter. It all tasted the same.

Jezebel got up from her seat and joined me in the back, her replacement drug of choice being a chocolate glazed doughnut instead of coffee. She was a middle-aged woman with curly blonde hair and forty extra pounds. She had deep lines around her eyes, a testament to the struggles she'd endured in her life. I could relate to struggles. We'd partnered up the week before—a natural fit.

"I didn't know you fancied yourself as a public speaker," she said before ripping off a bite of her doughnut.

"I don't, but it's not something that scares me."

"There are a lot of people who think public speaking is worse than death."

"It's not; trust me," I said with an amused grin.

"I know it sucks to always feel like you're starting over, but each threshold you reach does get a little easier. You just can't see it yet. I never thought I could make it to my first year, and here I am before you today, nearly five years sober." When she smiled, I could still see chocolate on her teeth. "It's good you're getting control of this while you're still young. It gets so much harder as you get older—take my word for it. I commend you for your bravery. I would have thought this was court mandated, from a DUI or something."

"I've got a lot to learn from you," I said with a smile as I finished my coffee, then crushed the paper cup and tossed it in the trash.

"Stick with me, kid. I'll get you to the other side."

"I have no doubt," I said, and we walked back to our chairs and listened to others share for the remainder of the session. Then I received my thirty-day chip along with two other attendees.

As soon as I left the church activity center, an adjacent building to St. Paul's Cathedral, thoughts of Fiona flooded back. Walking across the parking lot in the relentlessly warm sun, I reached my hand into my pants pocket and held the chip like it would give me the strength I needed to continue with what needed to be done. I'd never thought this would be so hard. The need was welling up inside me—the hunger that never went away—only amplified as I pictured Fiona. She was important, and I had to rise above my primal urges.

My phone buzzed in my opposite pocket. "Do you have an update?" I asked, getting right to the point.

"Not on the cause of the accident," Jack said, my trusted associate at Sisters of Mercy. I had him looking into the mysterious coyote sighting that caused Fiona's boyfriend to crash. I was confident this was no mere accident—but a deliberate attempt on her life. I could guess who was behind it, but wanted definitive proof before retaliating.

"Okay; then what's up?"

"Fiona made the call," Jack said.

I couldn't suppress a smile. I knew she would, but

hadn't expected her to do it so soon. I knew I shouldn't be so happy about this, but couldn't help myself. "Thank you for the update. It's shaping up to be a beautiful day."

10

FIONA

"We're sorry; you have reached a number that has been disconnected or is no longer in service. If you feel you have reached this recording in error, please check the number and try your call again," an automated voice said over the phone.

I called the number at least ten more times that morning to make sure I had dialed it correctly, but every time I received the same aggravating message.

I was furious, but mostly at myself for starting to get my hopes up. I'd repeatedly told myself not to have expectations in searching for my father. I thought I had been doing a good job with that, but Sean obviously hadn't felt the same way. So, we'd agreed to disagree, but that wasn't going to salvage our relationship. I didn't know if this current phone issue was some kind of accident or an official renege of my invitation. I felt so stupid.

It wasn't until after a full day of scolding myself that I remembered Matthew's business card. He had been there in the glass room and may have even been involved with my abduction—and he had given me a business card with another phone number. After my Sunday afternoon shift at Hot Coffee, I told Candace I couldn't hang out with her for break and rushed home to grab the card from my nightstand. But halfway through dialing, I realized the numbers looked familiar, causing me to stop and compare the two cards.

The stupid phone numbers are the same! I groaned and finished dialing, only to be tormented by the same message.

"We're sorry; you have reached a number that has been disconnected or is no longer in service..."

I threw both cards into the nightstand drawer and collapsed onto my bed with a sigh. I wanted to yell at Becca for convincing me to call, but knew that wouldn't do any good. It wasn't her fault; I would've come to the same conclusion on my own. I was just so upset I'd started to believe that my search actually *was* over. Maybe this was all some elaborate prank anyway and never would have led anywhere. The more I lay in despair, cursing my luck, the more I began to consider talking to Mallory Fiennes— something I absolutely dreaded doing.

Of course, I could never find her alone at school. Mallory was always surrounded by her fans and admirers, desperate people craving a little bit of her popularity to rub off on them. She was pretty, wealthy, and bitchy—seemingly the perfect concoction of important characteristics to become a popular girl in high school. Clichés were clichés for a reason. And the mean girl cliché didn't stop Mallory Fiennes from being arguably the most popular person. But who was counting?

I finally got so desperate that I followed her into the bathroom after leaving a class we shared. We wouldn't be alone, but at least the two friends she was walking with continued to their next classes while Mallory stopped off.

I waited a good thirty seconds before entering, so it didn't *look* like I was following her. I also didn't know if she really had to go or was just fixing her makeup. When I got inside, I scanned the other girls at the row of sinks. Mallory was not among them.

I guess she had to go.

All the stalls were already taken and there was now a line of two girls waiting, so I headed over to a free sink, set my backpack on the edge, and fished out my compact to dull the irritating sheen forming on my brow.

The multiple conversations surrounding me quickly became senseless chatter, but Mallory's voice always had a way of piercing through the noise.

"Frankenstein had fewer blemishes to conceal," she said, appearing one sink over, already drying her hands.

"Frankenstein's monster," I corrected. "Frankenstein was the mad scientist."

"You would know," she shot back, dabbing at her eye makeup, making sure it was perfect—which it was.

I let out a long breath, trying to keep my blood from boiling, then turned to her and made sure to keep my tone civil. "That card we received from those—" I glanced around the bathroom, then stepped closer to Mallory before continuing. "—those people claiming to be the True North Society… Did you call the number?"

"Are you seriously talking to me right now?" Mallory flashed me an annoyed glare.

"Yes; *I'm actually talking to you right now*. It's a free country," I argued, which I immediately knew was shooting myself in the foot.

"Then feel free to cut your other cheek, so you're at least symmetrical." She smirked at me and walked off, the other girls around clearing a path for her all the way to the door.

Snickers and whispers reached my ears while I remained standing at the sink, trying to find my composure. I wanted to scream, but instead adjusted my bangs in the mirror, then stormed out of the bathroom. I had known it was a mistake to try and talk to her. But what else could I do?

I didn't have many choices other than try and forget about what I'd seen and heard—all about Matthew and the True North Society—and get on with my life, one mailed letter and one new house visit at a time.

AFTER SCHOOL, Alexis drove me to work. We were both closing the store as normal, with Candace already here as our pre-closer. Now that the three of us were together, the elephant in the room was the incident at Black Star Canyon that neither of them could yet explain. Of course, I could explain it but had to continue playing dumb.

"You know the strangest thing about that night?" Alexis asked as she sat next to me, running a finger through the condensation on her glass. "The fact that none of us remembers anything after building the fire… unless someone is hiding something." She glanced over at me, eyes pleading for more information.

"Don't look at me," I scoffed. "I could ask you the same question."

"You're right."

"That's why I'm telling you we need to sue the manufacturer," Candace said from the bar. "Our drinks were sealed, but there was something in them."

"What are you girls talking about?" Eli asked, coming out from the office. "Someone slipped you a roofie?"

"*No!*" Alexis said, sounding incredibly offended, which killed the conversation right there.

"Okay; calm down. Sorry I asked," Eli said and stopped at the register to greet a customer perusing the pastry case.

"At least we're all okay, right?" Alexis said, her attention back on her glass.

"That's the important thing," I said and took a frothy sip of my white mocha. The more I spoke about the situation, the guiltier I felt.

"I'm never drinking again," she said without a hint of sarcasm, making me laugh. Alexis glared at me for making light of her statement. "I'm serious, Fee. Don't you feel the same way?"

"Sorry; I probably lack the conviction you do, but agree we need to be more careful."

"I'm always careful, but things got out of control anyway. I just don't understand."

"Can we just drop it, please?" I seriously didn't want to keep talking about this. It wasn't like we were getting anywhere.

"Right. Never talk about it again," Alexis said, sounding hurt. "Denial is the best policy."

"I'm not in denial, I just don't want to dwell."

"Are you kidding? Alex lives to dwell," Candace said, rounding the back of the pastry case.

"And you live to deny," Alexis argued.

"Plausible deniability is a valuable skill, and I won't *deny* I use it to my advantage." Candace was about to take a seat on the prep counter, but noticed Eli eyeing her and thought better of it. "I was just testing you," she said with a smirk.

Alexis hopped down from her stool and pulled the strap of her apron over her head. I noticed it was time for our shift and hurried to finish my white mocha. As soon as I vacated my bar stool, my phone started buzzing in my jeans pocket.

The screen displayed *Private Number*, which I would typically never answer. But I had to know—had to know who it was after my repeated failed attempts to reach the True North Society.

"Hello?" I answered hesitantly, almost expecting to hear the beginning of a prerecorded message. But I was greeted with a live human voice.

"Fiona Winter?" the deep male voice asked.

"Yes. Who's this?"

"This is your callback. If you wish to continue, then return to the location you were originally picked up. Friday night. 11 p.m."

"Then what?"

"Wait. You'll receive further instructions there. But be warned—we will *not* wait, and you will *not* receive another call. Do you understand?"

I understood the words the mysterious man was speaking, but not what was really going on. I wanted to ask more questions, get further clarification, but Eli was giving me the look that it was time to clock in.

I cupped my hand around the phone and lowered my voice. "You're with the True North Society, right?"

But instead of receiving an answer, the line went dead.

11

FIONA

J took an Uber to the closest shopping center before entering the canyons, then walked the rest of the way. Luckily, I remembered to bring a flashlight, since once I left the main road, there was nothing left to guide my way but moonlight. I waited by the gate where we always parked whenever we came to Black Star Canyon.

It was a quarter past eleven when bright headlights came inching their way up the gravel road. When the vehicle stopped ten feet from where I was sitting on the gate, the driver's door opened, and Matthew stepped out wearing a black suit.

"Hello again, Fiona Winter," Matthew said, my name sounding so sweet on his lips. He definitely hadn't been the one who called me.

"Hello again, Matthew Mercer," I said, looking him over as he stepped into the headlights.

He glanced around into the open darkness, then his eyes landed back on me. "This is a long way to walk."

"I did what was necessary to get here," I said.

"And as your reward, you get the privilege of sitting in the front seat with me." Matthew produced a smile as bright as the xenon headlights.

"Wow; that *is* a privilege," I said sardonically. "No injection this time?"

"No needles," Matthew answered. "We should get going; don't want to be late."

I nodded and made my way toward the passenger front seat of the SUV. When Matthew took his spot in the driver seat, he said, "Two things before we go. First, hand me your cell phone."

I didn't protest, pulling out my phone and passing it to him. Matthew opened the center compartment, placed my phone inside, then pulled out a black eye mask with a rubber band back. He dropped it in my lap.

"What's this?" I asked.

"A blindfold," he said. "I thought it was pretty obvious."

"I realize that," I said. "But when you mentioned no injections earlier, I assumed it meant I could see where we were going."

"Well that was your first mistake. Never assume. Now if you'd be so kind, please put on the blindfold, so we can go."

I let out an exaggeratedly annoyed breath and did what I was told. "I had hoped we were past this by now. I've been chosen and I accepted."

"You're accepting to be a candidate. You're not being initiated. You have a bit of a process ahead of you before reaching that point. We need to be cautious, like President Bolt said."

Matthew made a three-point turn to get back to the main road, turned sharply, then sped away. I really wanted to peek through the bottom of the blindfold, but felt Matthew watching me and didn't want him to have to take *extra precautions*.

"How far is it to get to where we're going?" I asked.

"It's about a 45-minute drive," he said. "Reception gets spotty in places, so I'll play music from my phone. Got any requests?"

"Anything you're into, I'm sure will be fine… Unless it's like polka or something. Is that what you like? I don't want to offend you."

"How about some Top 40?" he asked, but it wasn't really a question. He turned up the volume and it started with a Charlie Puth song. The music quickly consumed the whole inside of the leather-trimmed vehicle.

When we reached our destination, he came over and opened my door, took my hand, and led me into some mysterious building. Once inside, he slid the blindfold off my head and placed it in a pants pocket. A few of his fingers brushed my cheek in doing so—right over the scar—and left a trail of hot skin behind.

If I didn't know any better, I would have sworn this was an office building at 9 o'clock on a Monday morning, with everyone rushing to get stuff done. From an outsider, it just looked like chaos.

Matthew guided me down several flights of stairs like we'd come in on the top floor, then continued down a labyrinth of hallways. The lower levels of the building were quieter than where we'd arrived. Then he stopped outside of a nondescript door.

Matthew opened the door and flipped on the lights. I peered into an unoccupied office. There was a large wooden desk, bookcases with rows and stacks of books, and a taller table with blueprints of some kind. A long, flowing, formal red dress was hanging from a coat hook. There was also a shoebox on the floor directly below it.

"What is this?" I asked.

"Time for you to get changed," Matthew said.

"Seriously?" I asked, glaring at him. *You've got to be kidding me.*

"I'll wait right outside." He lifted his sleeve and tapped his wrist like he was wearing a watch and time was of the essence—and while he performed the irritating gesture, I noticed the edges of a large tattoo on the underside of his forearm. "You have five minutes."

. . .

THE OFFICE HAD AN EN-SUITE BATHROOM. I stared at myself in the mirror, seeing myself in the flowing red dress. The skirt nearly brushed the floor, even with the silver open-toed heels I was given. The corset was tight with crisscrossing lace in the back. There was a V-neckline, with sleeves off the shoulders. Besides the scar down my right cheek, there was another large scar on my right shoulder from where the dog had ripped a chunk out of it, trying to pull me. This was the reason I never showed off my shoulders in public. But in truth, despite my bodily imperfections, the dress fit perfectly and looked like it could have been worn by a celebrity on the red carpet. It made me look like a woman—albeit a slightly damaged one—even with my flat hair and minimal makeup just comprising of foundation, mascara, and nude lip gloss. I pinched my cheeks for color, knowing full well it wouldn't last.

Now, the ability to walk gracefully was another matter altogether.

I met Matthew at the door; he took in all of me with his smoky gray eyes filled with what almost looked like desire. I quickly found myself blushing uncontrollably.

"You look… you look incredible," Matthew said.

I reflexively freed my bangs from behind my right ear and put a hand on my shoulder to cover-up the exposed scar, but he reached for my hand and removed it.

"No; don't do that. You're beautiful just the way you are," he said, tucked my bangs back behind my ear, and traced a knuckle along the palpable line running down my cheek.

I flinched at his touch, but again, didn't pull away like I'd done to everyone else in the past. Even Sean knew better than to touch my scars.

"There's just one thing missing."

"Oh yeah? What's that?" I asked, actively restraining my hand not to adjust my hair or re-cover my ugly shoulder.

He reached into his suit coat pocket and pulled out a black felt jewelry box. He opened the lid and presented the little box to me.

Inside was a white gold necklace with a compass pendant, diamond accents, and an "N" of rubies.

"Are these real?" I asked with a slight gasp.

He nodded as he removed the necklace from the box.

I turned around and lifted my hair so he could place the chain around my neck. When I turned back, he was looking at me in that way again, making me feel elated, tingly, and uncomfortable all at the same time—all feelings that labored my breathing.

"There," he said. "Now you're ready."

Instead of subjecting me to more stairs, Matthew

led me to an elevator, which really helped in the high heels. He took my arm and looped it through his elbow, making us look like a couple ready for prom or a wedding. I felt the eyes of everyone we passed in the halls, not overly comfortable in this formal attire.

After a few more turns and hallways, we entered a door that said, *Backstage*. It was dark, and we passed by what looked like a lot of random junk: boxes, stacked chairs, rows of curtains, ropes extending into the rafters, and strewn-about musical instruments.

Matthew held back a curtain to let me through and I found myself on a large stage with the other three candidates. A towering burgundy curtain separated the stage from whatever auditorium lay beyond. And all was quiet.

Of course, Mallory Fiennes was there. Naturally, she greeted me with a glare of contempt, but the other candidates seemed almost happy to see me. They were all dressed just as elegantly as I was, and the girls had the same ruby and diamond pendant at their throats.

Numbers had been taped to the stage floor, and Matthew told me to stand on the number three. Mallory's spot was directly to my left on number four and she seemed even more unhappy about that.

"That dress sure accentuates your flaws," she whispered without turning her head toward me.

"Excuse me?" I said, even though I'd heard her loud and clear. It hurt, but I tried not to let it show—not to give her the satisfaction of getting under my skin.

"You shouldn't have come."

"I have just as much right to be here as you." I continued looking straight ahead, out at the burgundy curtain.

"We'll see about that."

Matthew was talking with some soldiers on the far side of the stage and glanced over a few times.

I ran my fingers through my hair and made sure my right cheek was covered. The shoes themselves were comfortable, but I still oscillated my weight between feet. I didn't know how long we'd be standing here. At least I knew enough not to lock my knees. I didn't know if I was sweating more from my nervousness or the overhead lights.

After a few minutes of standing in silence, the soldiers walked off the stage.

Matthew came over to me first. "You're going to be fine," he said before joining the soldiers offstage.

Then it was just the four of us in the middle of the immense stage before the towering burgundy curtain, under the blazing lights. Other than some inconspicuous fidgeting, nobody moved. The whole room was silent. Nobody dared talk.

Suddenly, the overhead lights went out and we were shrouded in complete darkness. What

surprised me more was the applause that followed—
and not just applause, but thunderous applause that
drowned out all my immediate thoughts. While I
heard the curtain parting, the strings segment of an
orchestra began playing somewhere below us. The
assortment of strings was soon accompanied by
wind instruments, and then drums, quickly building
to a crescendo. The thunderous applause grew even
louder.

Blinding spotlights suddenly shone down on
each of us, finally giving me a glimpse of how grand
this auditorium was that stretched out before us—
and it was completely full. Rows extended back into
darkness. There were tiers and balconies, every seat
in the house filled, and now those men and women
in half-masks, tuxedos, and formal gowns were up
on their feet, applauding—all for us.

12

FIONA

*T*he music died down, but the applause continued as the seven masked figures in black robes entered from the side of the stage. A separate spotlight shone on the figure with the strange bird mask—who last time had claimed to be the president of the True North Society and of some other world organization. It followed her as she floated to the center of the stage. She raised up both gloved hands. The roar subsided to a murmur and the audience took their seats.

"Welcome, esteemed Society members and friends." She spoke into a hand-held microphone. "Many of you traveled many miles to be here tonight —on this momentous occasion—to witness and celebrate the newest pledging of candidates into the True North Society. We have members joining us from all fifty states and forty-six nations around the world. I am honored and humbled that all of you could be here this evening. I thank you," she said and held her free arm out in a sweeping gesture. "And to the future candidates, thank you."

She turned to us to continue her speech. "I know that you did not make this decision lightly and I hope you are ready to work."

I didn't know what she meant by work, but I already had quite a lot of work between school and the coffee shop. I gulped at what she was insinuating.

"The trials on the road to initiation that I mentioned last time will not be trivial, they will not be easy, and they will not be without purpose. They will test you physically, emotionally, and will test your sense of commitment to this unique institution. I don't want to scare you, but I want to prepare you —prepare you for anything, because that is what it will take. All four of you are coming from very different backgrounds, social standings, educational levels, work experiences, and life experiences.

"Barry, I know you're joining us all the way from Virginia.

"Zelda, you're joining us from Nevada.

"And Mallory and Fiona, you're both coming to us from our own backyard.

"You are all very different and your opportunities, too, will be different, dependent on your expertise and skill levels. But there is no shortage of opportunity, home and abroad—and my usage of *abroad* is probably a little different than yours, which you'll discover in due time. Last time, I said that the True North Society did not exist. That is true and yet it's also not true. Over the past fifty years, the True North Society has infiltrated every major government, agency, research facility, and financial and informational institution in the United States. And over the past two decades, that has spilled over into the global arena. There are major works in effect right now, and if you reach initiation, you, too, can be a part in what's being built—you, too, can be a part of history.

"You will each be given an aid to help you through the candidate process. The person standing behind you will be your coach and be with you every step of the way. But your coach can only do so much. You have to take their direction and advice and prepare yourself as much as possible."

I didn't want to glance over my shoulder to see who would be standing behind me since I'd never heard anyone approach. The only person I knew was Matthew, so I hoped it was him. But I knew better than to get my hopes up.

"Now, I must require your verbal consent that you want to move forward. This is a life-changing event—a calling that will define the rest of your lives and I must insist you actively proclaim your desire to proceed."

The president walked over to Barry on the number one spot and held out the microphone.

"I do," he said, his voice booming throughout the auditorium.

Zelda stood on the number two spot, so she was the next to speak up. "I do."

Before I knew it, all eyes were on me. I thought I was frightened the first night, but after everything the president had said about life-changing events, I was more than petrified, not knowing what I had truly gotten myself into. But with all these eyes staring at me, I was somehow even more afraid to back down and not follow the precedent set by the candidates who'd spoken before me.

"I do," I said, and my voice cracked right in the middle of the short phrase.

The president nodded at my weak reply, seemingly satisfied with it, and moved on to Mallory, who gave her bold acceptance.

"Just because you are not privileged to learn the great secrets of this institution just yet, we value our candidates as much as our fully initiated members. Some doors will remain locked until you are initiated, but the doors open for you now are fully open. We are all sisters and brothers and we rest our lives in each other's hands. We are bound by the very survival of human existence and no other group on Earth can make such a proclamation.

"So, before you leave today and start your

journey as a candidate of the True North Society, you will be bound in blood to signify that we are all one."

Two other figures stepped forward from the cluster of seven in robes—the one with the red devil mask and the one with the white wolf mask. They walked over to a small wooden table positioned by the edge of the stage. One of the spotlights followed them. On the table was a crystal decanter with some type of dark liquid inside, a golden chalice, a large stone basin with a neatly folded towel beside it, a clear pitcher filled with what looked like water, and a double-bladed dagger.

The figure with the devil face picked up the golden chalice and the figure with the wolf face picked up the dagger.

My heart began to beat heavier and faster as they approached. And as they did, the large audience in the auditorium rose. They were going to start with Mallory, who didn't look quite as confident anymore.

"Hold out your left hand," the man with the wolf face commanded.

She hesitated, but soon did as she was bid.

With his free hand, the man with the wolf face turned her hand palm side up, then held it steady. He brought the tip of the dagger to her palm.

"Bound in blood. Bound as one," he said and slid

the dagger across Mallory's palm; immediately, the blood began to flow.

"Bound in blood. Bound as one," the audience and remaining figures onstage boomed in unison.

Mallory clenched her hand and held it over the golden chalice. Crimson droplets splashed into it. When a small puddle had formed, the figure with the devil face handed her a white hand towel from beneath his cloak, and they both moved on to me.

"Hold out your left hand," the man with the wolf face repeated.

Instead of holding it out, I clenched both hands tightly into fists. All the muscles going up my arms tensed as I stood there, frozen.

The man with the wolf face repeated his command, slower this time.

I felt a nudge from behind, and someone whispered in my ear. "It's okay."

I recognized the voice as Matthew's which succeeded in slightly calming my nerves.

I reluctantly unclenched my fists and lifted my left arm, knowing to have my hand palm up.

The man with the wolf face held my hand steady as he brought the tip of the dagger to my overly sensitive and exposed skin.

"Bound in blood. Bound as one," he said and slid the blade across my palm, leaving a red trail in its wake.

"Bound in blood. Bound as one," everyone shouted in unison, even louder this time.

Like Mallory, I was instructed to ball my hand into a fist and hold it over the golden chalice. Warm blood dripped from my extended hand and mixed with hers.

As I gazed into the small pool of blood, I felt a cold sweat creeping to the surface of my skin. The overhead lights seemed to dim. My head suddenly became increasingly heavy. And then the stars came out.

Oh no...not now.

"You don't look so well," Mallory said with mocking concern.

The figure with the devil mask was offering me a towel for my hand, but I wasn't concerned with stopping the bleeding any longer.

Don't lock your knees.

Everything was quickly fading to black. I reached out only to find open air.

"I've got her," a voice said, but I couldn't distinguish whose.

I was already falling.

MATTHEW

*B*y the time Fiona awoke, I had a pillow under her head and a damp towel on her forehead.

She gazed up at me incredibly confused, then the events of the last few minutes must have hit her. She soon realized my hand was in hers, applying pressure with a fresh towel to the gash across her palm. Blood left dark splotches on the new dress, splashes on the silver shoes, and patches on the floor around us. I tried to keep my focus on her worried face.

The assemblymen tasked with the binding ritual were now in front of Barry.

President Bolt in the plague doctor mask was watching us intently. I knew she was skeptical of Fiona being admitted into the Society due to criticisms and lobbying from other members of the assembly, and this certainly wasn't helping—it wasn't helping her cause and mine for insisting on being her coach, something I'd only done once before.

Fiona looked mortified, like she wanted to cry, but didn't. Her hand was trembling in mine, but she was determined to remain strong.

"It's okay," I whispered. "I've got you. You will get past this."

"Are you sure?" Fiona whispered back. "They're all still looking at me, aren't they?"

"You can't quit now, so you might as well get back on your feet and fight."

"Who says I can't quit."

"I do."

"Bound in blood! Bound as one!" The thunderous declaration shook the entire stage floor.

"I will never be bound to the likes of you," Mallory said subtly over the storm.

"Then you won't get in," I shot back at her.

My comment made Fiona smile, but amidst this small joy, tears finally began to spill down her cheeks. She didn't bother to wipe them away. Instead, she glared back at Mallory as she sat up, and then with a little help from me, gradually rose to her feet. In the process, she kicked off her shoes and stood barefoot between the other candidates, defiantly standing in her own blood.

The assemblyman with the wolf face, still standing before Barry, brought the blade of the dagger to his own palm, sliced it without hesitation, and spilled the blood into the chalice to mix with the contributions from the candidates. He presented his maimed hand to everyone before covering it with another white hand towel.

I hadn't been a part of this ceremony in over fifty years, and all this now reminded me of why. I did my best to keep my attention off all the blood.

This wasn't a good idea...

Afterward, the assemblyman with the devil face and the other with the wolf face walked back to the table at the edge of the stage. The wolf-faced one washed the blade of the dagger in the basin using water from the pitcher, then set it on the table. The devil-faced man poured the dark liquid into the chalice, then carefully swirled the contents.

The two men returned to the candidates, this time with only the filled chalice between them. Again, they stopped at Mallory first.

"Drink," the assemblyman with the devil face said, offering her the golden cup. "Drink and be one," he said, and the chorus of a thousand followed.

"Bound in blood. Bound as one," the crowd roared.

Mallory took the cup, which shook ever so slightly in her hand. The audience wouldn't have been able to see her fear, but I could—and I was pretty sure Fiona noticed it too. After a glance over at Fiona and me, she took a sip so small, I wasn't sure if she actually drank anything at all and handed the chalice back to the red devil assemblyman.

I knew she was going to try to get away with as much as she could, just like her father and brother, which had always been a pet peeve of mine. But I was bound to them too, so we all had to ultimately work together.

Both men stepped to Fiona and presented her with the chalice. She seemed so much shorter and smaller now that she was standing before them barefoot, the ominous figures of the assemblymen overshadowing her.

She took it with her non-injured hand, peered inside and made a face. I could only guess what she was thinking, probably afraid she'd gotten herself into some vampiric cult, aiming to sacrifice her. I knew she could ultimately handle the truth when it was finally presented, but I feared her reaction in the short term.

"Drink and be one," he said, and the audience repeated.

"Bound in blood. Bound as one."

The chalice shook in her hand as she raised it to her lips. Both men stared at her intently, just as critical as President Bolt had been. She took a sip—tentative, but a real sip, unlike Mallory. She coughed as she lowered the chalice and handed it back to the assemblyman with the devil mask.

He took the chalice from her, nodded, and

systematically moved on to Zelda. She drank willingly, as did Barry. I could see Fiona visibly relax her shoulders, though she was still struggling with a cough.

"Keep it down," I whispered into her ear.

She nodded, her uninjured hand still at her mouth.

"You're doing fine," I said and patted her on the shoulder.

I knew she didn't believe me, but all I could do was continue to reassure her—keep her from running out on the whole thing, thinking it was all a big mistake. I knew she wouldn't in the end but figured I would be playing an important role in keeping her here and on track.

"There," President Bolt said when the devil and wolf returned to the cloaked group. "Now we are all bound as one and it is time to begin. I wish you the best of luck during your training and trials, and I will see you again upon your completion—at which time I will congratulate you, remove my mask, and shake your hand. Until then, follow the directions of your coaches and remember you were chosen for a reason. Believe in yourself first. Everything else will follow."

When the president finished her speech, all the spotlights went out at once. The curtain came together and the seven masked figures sank back into the shadows from which they came. Overhead lights came on once the cloaked figures had departed. Everything was quiet again.

I hurried to retrieve more towels and began mopping up the mess on the stage floor. I needed this blood gone. It was not safe—for anyone.

"At least let me help you," Fiona said.

"Take care of your hand for now. I've got this," I said. "You should probably go sit down. I don't want you fainting again."

"I'm fine now," she insisted.

Mallory dabbed the tip of one shoe in a small puddle of Fiona's blood and drew a long merlot smear along the floor. "*So gross.*"

Aaron, her coach, guided her away before any more blood was spilled. I was tempted to do the honors, but knew how much I had to control my anger. Fiona looked a little murderous as well, which helped my composure.

Instead of taking a seat at the back of the stage, Fiona walked up to the closed curtain, found the overlap, and peeked into the auditorium. I knew she'd find it mostly empty by now. We had our ways of making it look like magic. She was shivering by the time she let the curtain fall back into place.

Once the stage was clean, I led her back to the hallway. Barry, Zelda, and their coaches were talking. Mallory and Aaron had left as soon as possible, as I'd expected. I introduced Fiona to who was left: Barry and Mac—Barry's coach—and Zelda and

Anderson, who was Zelda's coach. These candidates had been on our radar for some time, Fiona and Mallory since they were young; they had only recently turned eighteen. Barry and Zelda were found to fill specific recent gaps in our organizational structure. And what the candidates didn't know was that this would be the last candidate class the True North Society would ever have.

"I hope you're all ready to get real cozy together," Mac said with a laugh. "You guys will be going through a lot together... that is, if you make it through, of course."

"Where did the other girl go?" Zelda asked, obviously referring to Mallory.

"She's a special breed," I said.

"Look who's talking," Anderson commented, not maliciously, but I still gave him a warning glare.

"How are you feeling?" Barry asked Fiona.

"Better now," she said, her cheeks starting to flush again. "There's just something about my own blood and sharp objects."

"Hopefully, this was the worst of it," Zelda said.

The other coaches shared glances and knowing smiles. *The worst of it?* This was just the beginning.

"Barry, you're coming from a long way," Fiona said, desperate to change the subject and get the attention off herself.

"Yeah; I was warned—the second time," Barry said, eying his coach.

"You'll love it here," Mac said with a smirk and clapped his candidate on the shoulder. "Sunshine and a mild seventy-two degrees every day. What's not to love? Right, Matthew?"

"Most people can't complain," I said. "Let's get you guys cleaned up."

14

FIONA

The three of us candidates were led up a few flights of stairs and into what looked like a doctor's office. Inside, there was a young guy who looked somewhere above twenty, wearing khaki pants and a seaweed green polo shirt. He had pale, pointy features and straight black hair combed to one side.

"Hey, Kelly," Mac said. "I didn't think you'd be in here this late."

The guy stared at me a little too long before glancing at the rest of the group and addressing Mac. "Yeah, well... when duty calls."

"We'll stay out of your way," Anderson said, heading toward the supply cabinet and retrieving some medical supplies.

"The branding ceremony," Kelly said, taking a look at my hand. "That's not its official title, but it's what I like to call it. It looks like they got a little carried away with you." He was looking at my soiled dress...or maybe just me wearing it.

"This is Kelly. One of our infirmary techs," Matthew said, standing close to me.

"I do a lot more than that, but whatever," Kelly said. "I can take care of this one." He looked nervously at Matthew, like he was asking for permission.

"You're the expert," Matthew said. "You should probably do all of them since you're here."

Anderson dropped the medical supplies on a nearby mobile table. "Knock yourself out, Kelly."

"These are our newest candidates—Barry, Zelda, and Fiona. There's one more, Mallory, but Aaron stole her away."

"So, you're the infamous Fiona," Kelly said, starting with me. He brought over disinfectant, bandages, and tape.

"I didn't know anyone thought of me as *infamous*," I said.

"That's just Kelly. He has a flair for the dramatic," Mac laughed.

Kelly gave Barry's coach a seething glare but didn't respond. He silently worked on bandaging my hand. "Did you upset someone? Your cut's deeper than normal," he commented as he finished wrapping my hand in gauze. "A few butterfly bandages will help it heal and reduce the scar."

"One more to add to the collection," I said, even though I didn't want to call more attention to my other markings.

"It shouldn't be too bad. Branding ceremony." Kelly showed me his left palm and the thin silver line stretching across it. "See? We all have to go through it."

I reached out and trailed a finger along his scar, then looked up at Matthew. "Let me see yours."

Matthew balled both hands into fists. "I don't have one," he said.

"You don't?" I asked. "But—"

"It was different for me," he snapped, like I had offended him.

"Sorry," I muttered and turned back to Kelly.

"You're good as new—well, almost," Kelly said and produced a warm, yet awkward smile. "Fiona, I can't get over it. You look so much like—" He suddenly stopped mid-sentence, now looking past me. "Like an old friend of mine," he said.

I glanced back at Matthew, who provided an innocent shrug. By the time I turned back to Kelly, he'd moved on to bandaging Zelda's hand.

"I should probably get you home," Matthew said to me while the other candidates were getting fixed up.

I agreed, rose from the stool I'd been sitting on, and shook the good hands of the other candidates. "It was nice meeting you guys."

Matthew put his hand on the small of my back and led me into the hallway. My skin tingled from his touch, yearning for it more when he took his hand away.

"I suppose you'll want to change first," he said as we made our way down the hallway, him having to slow down so I could keep up in heels.

"That would be appreciated," I said, desperately wanting a shower to rid myself of all the dried blood —but that was something I wanted to do in the privacy of my own home.

Matthew guided me back to the office I'd originally dressed in, and I speedily changed back into my clothes. I rinsed my face and arms, determined to make myself somewhat presentable in front of him. Gazing at myself in the mirror, back in my regular clothes, I almost couldn't tell if the fantasy was over or just beginning. My stomach was twisted in knots with anxiety and anticipation.

Your search is over. What did it really mean?

I hung up the soiled dress, once so elegant and striking, and returned the silver heels to their box. Upon rejoining Matthew in the hallway, I started to unclasp the necklace, but he stopped me.

"No; the pendant is yours," he said. "Usually the dress and shoes would be too, but… well, we won't try to salvage those. I'll get you another one."

"You don't have to do that," I insisted, but was rather excited by the thought.

"As you wish," he replied with a wry grin.

I wanted to take my comment back, but instead remained quiet and let my heart sink.

We traveled down a new hallway—his hand not on me this time—then Matthew hit the down call button at a bank of elevators. The nearest doors opened immediately.

We descended to level P3 and entered a sparsely lit parking structure. The ceilings were low and our footfalls echoed in the confined space. We marched down a row lined with seemingly identical darkly-tinted Land Rovers on either side.

Matthew removed a clicker from his pocket and lights flashed, accompanied by a double beep several vehicles away. I was used to still having to use an actual key for Mom's car, which was more than a little outdated.

I climbed into the passenger seat. "Do I need a blindfold this time?"

"Can I trust you?" He glanced over at me again with that burning intensity.

There wasn't much left in me to melt. *What's wrong with me?* "Absolutely," I said.

"Good," was his one syllable response before taking off and speeding through the parking structure.

Instead of heading up to ground level, Matthew drove into a tunnel that descended further. There were no outside lights for guidance or emergencies, just a blackness that seemed to extend forever.

It took at least five minutes to emerge from the tunnel and onto a winding road surrounded by trees. After another mile or so, we merged onto a more significant road with typical divider lines and signage. And a few more miles of driving led us to an armed checkpoint, where it seemed we would be leaving the mysterious True North Society compound.

The gate lifted and a guard armed with a machine gun waved us through. Matthew slowed as we drove over intimidating-looking traffic spikes.

I turned in my seat to gaze back at the entry checkpoint and saw a sign that stated: *Maximum Security Facility. Department of Corrections.* An electrified fence stretched from the checkpoint and disappeared into the trees.

What is all this?

It took approximately half an hour to reach my apartment complex. Matthew never had to ask me for directions. He drove directly up to the walkway that led to my front door like he'd been here a hundred times. Now, I was partially afraid he had.

He parked against the curb, then opened the center compartment. After removing my phone, Matthew apparently unlocked it before thumbing through the touchscreen and making some adjustments.

He knows my freakin' password too?

"There," he said, handing me back the phone. "Now you can really get a hold of me, and I, you. I'll expect you to answer when I call. Your candidacy is a serious obligation."

"What if I discover this really isn't for me?" I asked.

"We'll discuss that if it arises," Matthew said. "But I know what you've been searching for and I know we can provide you with the answers you seek."

"So, you can tell me about my father?"

"There are things you must learn before important doors can be unlocked. This is not just about me, but the organization as a whole. I would love nothing more than to tell you everything right now, but we all need to follow the proper protocol. You need to be provided the right context and your expectations must be managed appropriately. Believe me; we have a lot of work to do. But if you put in the time, I assure you, you'll get your answers... probably more than you bargained for."

"Now you're making me nervous."

"I'm sorry. There's no easy way to prepare you. We'll be taking one step at a time throughout your candidacy, but each step is monumentally high."

"I have to know," I said. "I'm ready."

Matthew gave me a sad smile. "And I'm ready to lead you into the dark, where all the answers have been hidden for years... generations... millennia.

Our time together will not be easy, but I'm looking forward to it."

I didn't really know how to respond, so I simply thanked him for the ride and unbuckled my safety belt—but my body still did not want to exit the car. Matthew was gazing at me with a sad, almost hungry look in his eyes. I could picture myself as his dinner, frozen in the tight confines of the front seat —him reaching across the center divider and pulling me closer—and some repressed part of me wanting him to take such a brazen action. There was an invisible force pulling my lips to his and I felt like it was affecting him too. I sat there, stock still in antic-ipation of his next move. I licked my lips to moisten them.

And the moment passed. He turned his attention back to the world outside the windshield. "You should go," he said softly. "It's about that transition from late to early."

My temper flared, feeling a stupid sense of rejec-tion. I exited the car without so much as another word. And he drove off with the same cold shoulder.

I searched my phone and found the contact he'd created. *Matthew Mercer.*

I felt childish for becoming angry with him after he'd just given me a ride home. This was another example of me expecting too much, something I knew not to do—and something he was now explic-itly telling me I mustn't. I shouldn't expect a man of his beauty, age, and sophistication to settle for a kid like me. And he was my new coach, for God's sake. It was stupid to get upset over this little fantasy.

My phone chimed and a message bubble popped up on the screen. I swiped the screen and clicked on the message icon, now overshadowed with the number one.

Good night, Fiona Winter, the message read. I didn't have to glance at the name to know who'd sent it.

A smile crept over my lips as I quietly snuck inside. I *so* needed to split an Oreo.

15

MATTHEW

J couldn't get my thoughts off all the blood on the stage floor. The fact it belonged to Fiona only made it that much worse. I'd been preparing for this a long time and was surprised how hard I was finding it now. She wasn't just any other candidate, but I should be able to treat her as such.

Why is this so damn hard?

My grip was so hard on the steering wheel, I was afraid I may crush it completely. I was losing control, my foot heavy on the accelerator. If I passed a cop, there'd be quite the pursuit because I'd have no intention of stopping. The Land Rovers were specially equipped—like police cruisers—but the Land Rovers had far superior power and technology. The police cruisers could corner better, but I could easily get around that with my driving skills.

I glanced down at the touchscreen of the info-tainment system and considered calling Jezebel. I needed a distraction to get Fiona out of my head—however temporary.

"Call Jezebel King," I said. Immediately, I received an automated response, then the sound of ringing streamed through the speakers as her name and number were displayed prominently across the touchscreen. But then her voicemail message began to play. "End call."

My foot became heavier on the accelerator as I raced into the foothills. My headlights were the only beacon in the darkness now. I hadn't passed a car in miles. There was nothing out here but desolate land-scape—rolling hills of rocks and tree husks. By the time summer hit, new greenery would emerge, just in time for everything to be burned down. Then the vicious cycle would start all over again.

Past the initial foothills, I wound up to a higher elevation, the small burned stubs giving way to larger trees until the sky had disappeared as I continued through the thick canopy.

The True North compound was bordered by an electrified fence, equipped with sensors and cameras all the way around the top of the mountain. The checkpoint was guarded like the grounds within the compound, twenty-four hours a day. Drones provided close-up aerial surveillance, as well as accompanying satellite footage. There was nothing that happened within the borders of the compound that our people were not aware of.

I pulled up to the checkpoint and lowered my window. "Good evening, Reynolds. Smith."

"Good evening, Mr. Mercer," Reynolds, the closest border patrolman, said with a nod.

Smith saluted behind him.

The tire spikes up ahead retracted into the road, allowing me to safely continue. We didn't want anyone to have the ability to race through the check-point, including myself.

I sped away from it, not afraid of hitting any pedestrians up here. I needed to get home as quickly as possible, needing to dull my hyperactive senses from thoughts and vivid images of Fiona. Her bright and innocent eyes. That shining chestnut-colored hair. The scar streaking down her cheek like a perpetual tear. Her unwavering fight to find her father.

I parked in the underground structure with the rest of the company vehicles and navigated through the headquarters building—typically referred to as the North Building. No building was marked as having anything to do with the True North Society.

Outside, there were several other buildings and a vista point near the edge of the mountain where on a clear night you could see the bright lights of Los Angeles. During the day, you could see the Pacific Ocean, all the way out to Catalina Island.

I crossed the open grounds to the imposing structure of the penitentiary—Silverado State Prison. The large stone outer wall was two stories high and had only one gated entrance. The inner stone structure of the penitentiary was ten stories, the top of which had an even better view than the vista point. The criminal population there was small but reserved for the worst of the worst—the worst of the worst who were not considered high profile cases. The lifers and death row inmates you'd never heard of resided there on the first two levels.

As I walked toward the gate, it began to rise, operated by guards in one of the turret control stations. None met me at the entrance, allowing me to continue through the outer wall, cross the separated yard, and reach the main building. Floodlights remained on to light the grounds, but much of the lower levels of the penitentiary stood dark—the inmates knowing better than to make too much noise after nightfall.

Entering the prison, I passed through the metal detectors and security doors without incident; without stopping, I made my way to the emergency staircase, the only way beside the south freight elevator to get to the third floor. From there, I could take the regular civilian elevators to get to the top floor, where my apartment resided.

"Good evening, Peter," I said to the impeccably dressed elevator attendant.

"Mr. Mercer. Good evening to you, sir," he said, holding the door open to allow me to enter. "Returning home?"

"Indeed."

Peter hit the tenth-floor button with a white-gloved hand. "Can I call anything in for you, sir?"

"No; thank you. There's nothing I require right now."

"Very good, sir."

On departing the elevator, I strolled down the long hallway to reach my apartment, one of only ten on this top level of the penitentiary. Each unit here double the size of those on the floor below, which again were already quite a bit larger than the first few floors above the prison.

I stood before the retinal scanner, which unlocked the front door once my identity was verified. I heard the elevator ding as soon as I stepped into the apartment and closed the door. I didn't want to see another living soul until I was able to get my emotions under control—to get the vivid thoughts of Fiona out of the forefront of my consciousness.

But before I was able to do anything, there was a knock at my door.

I don't need this right now.

"What!?" I yelled, rubbing my temples.

"Matthew, please open the door," said a sweet, familiar voice. "Don't make me stand out here all night."

"Go away, Taylor," I warned. "It's not a good time."

"You haven't been returning my calls."

"Which isn't an invitation to show up at my door."

"You can't ignore me," she said, rapping her knuckles against the door again, making me cringe.

I squeezed my eyes shut, gritting my teeth, feeling like my head was about to explode. I stormed over to the door and flung it open. My finger was leveled right in her face, ready to tell her off, when I caught sight of her.

Taylor was a bombshell of a blonde, nearly six feet tall in stilettos, and not an inch of fat on her. She wore a long velvet coat that reached her knees, which hung open, the sash still swinging in midair. All she wore beneath the coat was gossamer black lingerie, a seductive play that would shatter the defenses of most men—but as appetizing as her lack of clothes was, it wasn't what made me see red.

There was a small cut on the left side of her neck, with blood dripping down, rolling over her shoulder, and trickling into the contour of her ample cleavage. Her hair was up in a tight bun, so there was no hiding the wound, which was fresh and continued to flow. She held a paring knife in her left hand down by her side, a knife that was still stained with her blood.

My pulse quickened to dangerous levels; my

willpower nearly nonexistent. "I—I told you it was… over…" I stammered.

"I know that's what you said," she said confidently. "But I don't believe that was what you meant." She took a step closer, and instead of stopping her right there, I backed up until she had fully entered the apartment.

"You need to leave," I said, but there was very little conviction behind my words.

"I'll leave once we've both had our fill," Taylor said, shutting the door and letting the velvet coat splash to the floor around her feet. She wiped two fingers through the stream of blood flowing from her neck and brought them to my lips. "I know what *you* need. And you know what *I* need. There's no use fighting it. I'm here for you."

As much as I wanted to wipe my mouth with my sleeve, I couldn't. I licked my lips and savored her sweet, familiar blood. And I couldn't stop myself from lunging forward, taking Taylor in my arms, and sinking my elongated fangs into her neck. Instantly, I was engulfed with true ecstasy, drinking deep from the nectar I'd been depriving myself of. And in that moment, I didn't care—I couldn't see or feel anything else, only the sweet morsel before me, docile and moaning in my arms as I continued to feed, eager to give me what she thought I needed.

Without severing our tie, I scooped up her fragile

body and carried her over to the couch to finish the job. Along the way, the paring knife dropped from her hand.

"Don't stop," she begged, which only fueled the frenzy. But we both knew I had to stop, or else I'd kill her. But knowing it and doing it were two entirely different things.

By the time I managed to pull away, she was unconscious on the couch, not a drop of her blood left on her mostly naked body. I watched the shallow rise and fall of her chest as I stood up and wiped my mouth with the back of my hand.

"Damn you, Taylor," I said, running my hands through my hair, then let out a scream. I couldn't even control that.

My phone buzzed in my pocket, which only made me more upset. I fished it out, ready to throw it against the wall, when I saw Jezebel's name on the screen. "Damn you too," I said before punching the answer button.

"Matthew, I saw I had a missed call from you. Is everything all right?" she asked, not sounding overly concerned.

"I—I couldn't stop myself," I said, my eyes still glued to the ravaged woman on my couch. "I gave into the urge and took a drink."

"I'm sorry I didn't answer earlier," she said. "I know it's disheartening with how well you've been doing. Temptation can cut down the best of us. You know that as well as anyone. You're only human, as are we all."

"Yes…" I said, unable to say anything more.

16

FIONA

"You got home late last night," Mom said when I got up.

Even though I had only gotten a few hours' sleep, it was all I could manage with my mind still reeling from the events of the night before. I didn't know how to properly process everything that had happened. Luckily, Becca had listened as I proceeded with the biggest info dump of my life. She didn't understand half of what I told her, but that wasn't the point. I just needed to say everything out loud. Even then, I hardly believed it myself.

"Oh my God, what happened to your hand?" Mom cried, looking up from her tablet and coffee.

I glanced down at my bandaged hand, with all the events of the ceremony flooding back to me, but tried to keep myself from being pulled down the rabbit hole. "Oh, it's nothing," I said. "I just cut myself preparing a sandwich last night."

"Does it need stitches? It'll scar worse if you just tape it closed."

I glared at her, but she didn't flinch. "You don't have to tell me that."

"Well, I don't know what it looks like. I'm just trying to help. I can take a look at it if you want."

"No, Mom. It's fine," I insisted and continued into the kitchen to start a new pot of coffee.

"It's still fresh," she said from the couch. "No need to dump it."

I dumped it nevertheless and brewed a new pot amidst adamant grumbling from the living room.

Once I had my coffee in hand and poured Mom a second cup, I curled up on the opposite side of the couch. Mom put down her tablet and repositioned herself to face me.

"You working today?" she asked.

"Yeah; you?"

She nodded. "But not until this afternoon. We should go out for lunch. When was the last time we went out together?"

"I dunno. It's been a while," I said.

"Precisely," she said. "The accident scared me to death, so I don't want this to come off insensitive or anything, but I loved spending the day with you after it happened. We haven't been spending time together. I don't want us to grow apart."

"We're not," I said. "We've just both been busy."

"Which means we need to make time for each other—schedule it. I don't want to deprive you of your friends, but I need some quality Fiona time too." Mom smiled and patted my knee.

"Lunch would be great," I said, placing my hand over hers. I could use the distraction, not wanting to simply sit around here.

THROUGHOUT LUNCH, I kept checking my phone for messages. I had it out every time I received a notification, most of which were junk that had nothing to do with me personally. I always got a few messages from Alexis or Candace throughout the day—and today was no different —but they were not the people I was hoping to hear from.

My mind continually wandered back to the final moments in Matthew's SUV, but in my thoughts, he reached over the center console and planted his full lips on mine.

"Fiona, are you and Sean okay?" Mom asked, stirring some sugar substitute into her iced tea with the straw.

Her question instantly brought my attention back to the table.

"You haven't mentioned him recently. I haven't heard you talking to him on the phone. You took all those pictures off your walls." She stopped, waiting for me to say something.

"Okay… we broke up," I said after a long pause.

"Did it have to do with the accident?"

"No; it actually happened before the accident." Her eyes had gotten so big and sorrowful, she almost forced me to look away to keep from breaking into tears. "It's okay, Mom. I'm okay. It wasn't some big dramatic thing. We hadn't seen eye to eye on certain things for a while and decided it was better to just go our separate ways now—before things got too serious."

"It already seemed like it was getting serious."

I shrugged. "I guess."

"Did this have anything to do with him accepting admission to NYU for next year?"

"No; it wasn't that."

"Because you still have a good chance of getting into Penn. It's only like two hours to New York City."

"I've already told you, I don't want to go to school on the east coast," I said. "I can't be that far from home."

"You don't have to worry about me," Mom said. "It would give me a good reason to get out there. I haven't been that far east since I was a little girl."

"*I know*, Mom." I probably sounded exasperated, even though I didn't mean to. As much as I wanted to be there for her—to keep our small family unit alive—I couldn't abandon Becca.

"Can I interest you both in any dessert?" the waiter asked, seemingly appearing out of nowhere. "I can personally vouch for the peach cobbler. You cannot get a better one in all of Orange County. Trust me; I've tried them all." He flashed us a brilliant smile of almost too-white teeth.

"Well, you've sold me," Mom said. "I wouldn't have even considered a peach cobbler thirty seconds ago, but now there's nothing I'd want more." She was laying it on pretty thick.

"And if you don't think it's every bit as good as I've promised, then it's on me." If his smile widened any more, it would have split his face in two. "How about you, miss? Would you like to join your sister in trying the best peach cobbler around?"

Now Mom was blushing. She loved the attention.

"I'll just steal a bite of hers," I said.

"Good luck with that," the waiter said as he removed our empty plates from the table, then glanced at Mom again before leaving our table.

"God, Mom; he's like twenty-five," I said, rolling my eyes.

"It's not like I'm gonna do anything about it." She slurped up the last of her iced tea. "You have to let an old lady like me have some fun once in a while."

Five minutes later, we were sharing a bowl of peach cobbler, digging into it with our own spoons.

Mom didn't have the heart to, but I told the waiter that our dessert was simply all right, so we could get it knocked off the bill. He seemed happy to do it—as well as adding his number to the receipt.

"I'm too old and you're too young," Mom said as she folded the receipt and stuffed it into her pocket. "I guess there's no justice."

"He's closer to my age than yours," I said sarcastically. "I'm legal now."

"Eww; don't say it like that, kid," she said.

I smiled at the nauseated face Mom made as we maneuvered past more servers and patrons, on our way to the door. I did miss this; it was a welcome distraction. I hadn't thought about Matthew or the crazy True North Society all through lunch.

Dammit.

MATTHEW

*I*didn't make it to Sisters of Mercy much anymore. The Operations Manager, Jack Nelson, took care of the day-to-day, so I could devote more of my time to the Society and other side projects. Jack was one of the natural born vampires I'd found in 1963 and brought to my adaption facility posing as a psychiatric hospital. I hadn't started it, but merely adapted it to my own vision when I took over. Jack had become a huge asset over the decades, as well as a close friend.

Like Jack, I was not given a choice with what I became, but my transition wasn't the gradual torment he'd been forced to endure, which was what made my facility so important. I could help people like him as they went through the multi-year transition from angsty teenager to vicious killer. The killer needed to be controlled, if he was going to live long in this repressed and paranoid world. And Jack was a testament to what this facility could accomplish.

The day crew was always minimal since the hospital functioned on reverse shifts—the hospital primarily being open and fully operational at night. There were only four other cars in the parking lot when I arrived, probably belonging to Jack and a few nurses. Jack wasn't typically here during the day, unless there was something he was working on for me.

I swiped my keycard to unlock the front door, anxious to get out of the hot sun, and strolled into the front reception area. I expected it to be unmanned and many of the lights to be off.

I walked by one of the patient rooms being cleaned by an orderly, the patient huddled on the bed in bloody rags from whatever activities she'd been subjected to the night before. She was no longer hurting, now simply afraid. I understood that fear—having experienced it myself many years prior—and it was important. It was a vital outlet for my kind in a safe space. I could admit that the treatment our human patients had to endure was cruel, but it was necessary for the greater good. The greater good was also an important concept for the Society—not simply in theory, but in practice. However, I knew that was a small consolation for the few confined within our haunted walls.

I continued to Jack's office and found him behind his desk with an open laptop, typing away at the keyboard.

"Knock, knock," I said, entering without an invitation and grabbing a seat on the opposite side of the desk.

"Let me send this email. I'm just about finished," Jack said, without looking up from the screen.

While waiting, I gazed around the room. This used to be my office, but when I turned over the primary operations to Jack, I gave him the office as well. I didn't need another place where I could store more junk. The few precious possessions I wanted to keep, I moved to my office in the North Building. Most of the items were specific to this facility, and the rest, I chucked.

"And sent," Jack said, not thirty seconds later. "Now let me bring up the videos." After more aggressive typing, he turned the screen of the laptop and came around the table himself, so he could view the video as well. "These originally came from a Snapchat feed before they expired. We haven't found any other footage popping up regarding the incident. Miraculously, the videos never made it to Facebook or Youtube, so it never went viral."

"Not like it would have been our problem anyway," I said. "We're not the paranormal police."

"I know, but we more often than not clean up messes set forth by the careless."

"When it protects our interests," I answered.

"Which this would have."

"True. But according to you, we don't have to worry about that," I said.

"So far, so good," Jack said and clicked the play button for the first video.

We watched what looked like a coyote trotting behind some trees and bushes lining a sidewalk. A thin voice could be heard, the voice of the girl shooting the video. "Look at the coyote. That's so cool! Never seen one in town before." But then the animal suddenly dashed across a multi-lane street, causing panic from several passing cars and the girl.

Cars were slamming on their brakes and swerving —among them a red Civic. I couldn't make out anyone in the car from the video's vantage point, but knew Fiona was in the passenger seat. The Civic did indeed strike the coyote as it fishtailed and veered off the road to avoid other vehicles. The body of the coyote bounced off the front bumper and skidded across the sidewalk, ultimately landing in a green belt away from the road. Then the Civic violently struck the light pole. The girl behind the video was shrieking now, partly in horror, partly in exhilaration of catching such a thrilling scene on video. The video cut off.

The next video picked up seconds later, focused on the coyote lying motionless in the grass. After some comments about the demise of the poor animal, it stirred from its slumber, then got back to its feet and limped away. It remained in the grass, following the sidewalk, as it now trotted behind trees along the way. The girl taking the video expressed her relief that the coyote had survived. Then it disappeared behind one tree and didn't emerge again. The video cut out once more.

The third video panned around the space where the coyote had been last seen, but had apparently vanished. The girl rationalized it had slipped into some nearby bushes without her realizing it, but then the camera stopped on a gaunt man in black pants and nothing else. He stood next to the tree where the coyote had last been seen, and he gazed out at the accident which had still not received the first emergency responders. The girl kept the camera on the shirtless, barefoot man, making childish comments about his toned physique.

"There's your guy," Jack said. "Do you recognize him?"

He looked familiar. I racked my brain for an identity or confirmed connection but couldn't come up with any. I shook my head. "I feel like I've seen him before, but I can't remember where. At least we've confirmed he's one of us. Now, we just need to find out who he is and who he's working for. I still say Frederick's behind this, but I don't want to retaliate until I'm sure."

"I'll keep digging," Jack said, returning the laptop to its original position on his desk.

"Thank you, my friend. Let me know as soon as you identify this guy. No one touches him but me. Since this involves Fiona, I insist on questioning him myself."

18

FIONA

I hadn't heard anything from Matthew or anything to do with the True North Society all weekend, forcing me to try and get back into my regular routine. My sole reminder was the white gold necklace with the compass pendant, which I continued to wear every day.

"When did you get this?" Candace asked as she held the pendant in her palm, forcing me to lean forward on the barstool.

"Yesterday," I said. "I went shopping with my mom."

"Good. You don't get enough stuff for *you*. I like it." She let the necklace go, allowing it to fall back between the open collar of my button-down blouse.

I took the final sip from my white mocha and slid the mug across the bar. Candace snatched it up and dropped it into the half-filled sink of other dirty dishes. She was waiting for me to come on shift, so I could wash them all. She despised drying out her hands. My skin wasn't as sensitive as hers, or maybe I just didn't let it get to me as much.

Eli emerged from the office and noticed me sitting at the bar. "I'm gonna take my lunch as soon as Fiona's clocked in," he said, then checked the timers on the coffee urns.

"Yes, sir," Candace said, sarcastically.

"Get off the counter," Eli scolded. "We shouldn't have to go over this every shift."

"Oh, come on, Mr. Fiennes never comes in this late."

"But his little minion does."

"Who cares about her?"

Alexis walked around from the espresso bar, approaching the resister. "Don't worry; I'll take care of all the customers."

"You're doing great, hun," Candace said, finally hopping down from the counter. "If you needed help, all you had to do was ask."

"It's your job to anticipate my needs."

"Oh, I'll *anticipate your needs*," Candace said, subtly spanking Alexis as she passed the register.

"Screw it; I'm going to lunch now," Eli said, sliding the supervisor keys across the bar, and marching out the door with a sigh.

I caught the slung keys and stretched their band around my wrist. I had a few minutes, but I might as well help out. I donned my apron as I threw my purse into the office, then joined Alexis and Candace out on the floor.

We worked in between playful banter while Eli was away. I had the keys to the store, so I was pseudo in charge, even though Candace had seniority. Eli would never give her the keys, even if she was the only other person on shift. We were always expected to be back on time, yet he rarely ever was. Even though Candace complained about it, we all enjoyed the extra unsupervised time.

"I'm in the mood for a *hot coffee*. What would you recommend?" a voice said from the bar.

Alexis was on register, Candace on bar, and I'd been floating between them to pass cups and retrieve food. I glanced over at the bar adjacent to the register and found a familiar face smiling at me, stopping me in my tracks.

"Matthew, what are you doing here?" I asked, a little breathless.

"I was in the neighborhood," he replied casually. "Thought I'd stop in and see what I was missing."

Alexis was now looking over, eyes wide, cheeks pinked.

"Only the best damn coffee in the county," called Candace from the bar. Then a few seconds later in a softer voice, "Sorry, ma'am. Didn't mean to curse."

Matthew chuckled, causing me to laugh as well.

"How about a simple dark roast? I'm not high maintenance."

"Then you don't want to know what I drink," I said, grabbing an overturned mug from atop the espresso machine.

"A medium three-pump, extra hot, extra whip white mocha," Alexis rattled off like an auctioneer.

I glared at her as I poured Matthew's coffee.

"That sounds terribly decadent," Matthew said, still smiling.

I placed his steaming mug on the bar before him and shrugged. "It's Candace's fault," I said.

"I heard that!" Candace said, already on her way over to us. "So, who's your friend?"

"This is Matthew," I said, trying to sound casual.

"Since when do you have a friend we don't know about?" Alexis asked, leaning against the register, her eyes still glued to Matthew. I could only guess what was running through her overanalyzing brain.

"He's... more of a family friend," I said. "Right, Matthew?"

"Yes; Fiona's mom, Susan, and I go back a few years. Our moms are friends—they used to work together. I just thought I'd stop in and say hi. Didn't think it would cause such an uproar."

"No uproar here," Candace said. "Just curious. Just talking. Casual conversation. So, what are your intentions with our friend?"

"Candace!" I whined, rolling my eyes.

"I have no intentions," Matthew said.

"She has a boyfriend, you know," Alexis added.

"I'm aware."

"I do not," I protested.

"Have you forgotten all about Sean?" Alexis asked, one hand settling on her hip.

"I'd forget about Sean with Matthew here," Candace said.

"Shut up. You're spoken for," I snapped.

Candace shrugged, giving me a pout, then returning a smile to Matthew.

Matthew sipped from his coffee, seemingly amused by the confrontational exchange.

"There's sugar and creamer in the lobby," Alexis said.

"You claim to have the *best damn coffee in the county* and want to mask its unparalleled taste with cream and sugar?" He used air quotes in reciting Candace's statement. "Sacrilege."

"Just because we got the best coffee around doesn't change the fact that plain black coffee sucks," Candace said like it was common knowledge. "You gotta spruce it up a little."

I tried to remain calm, but felt my heart racing in this man's presence like I was on caffeine overload. I could see just a hint of the smooth skin of his bare chest through the two open buttons of his dress shirt. His sleeves were rolled up to just below his elbows, revealing muscular forearms and a prominent tattoo on his inner left wrist. From the few lines I could see, it appeared to be a compass—like my pendant.

"Fee, you're staring," Candace said.

I snapped to attention, prying my eyes away from Matthew's captivating body. "I am doing no such thing," I protested, and in turning my head, saw Mallory standing silently in the lobby, an entourage of three more girls prattling quietly behind her.

The surprised look on my face got the attention of Alexis and Candace—and Matthew. Mallory looked almost apprehensive to approach the register. Her attention oscillated between Matthew and me, a strange, conflicting expression clouding her face.

"What may we get for you, *Your Highness*," Candace mocked, but Mallory barely noticed her, let alone reacted to her sarcasm.

After a moment, Mallory stepped up to the register and said, "I'll take my usual, and whatever my friends want." She had a credit card out and dropped it on the counter, then backed away so her friends could order.

Alexis was speechless, unsure if she should reach for the card.

"Eli's not back yet, so you're stuck with me," Candace said.

"I'm sure you'll have the decency not to spit in my chai," Mallory said.

"I'll try to control myself," Candace answered.

I turned my attention back to Matthew, who continued to casually sip his coffee. He didn't seem to pay Mallory any mind, even though I knew the feeling definitely wasn't mutual. She continued to glance over—an expression of disapproval forever present—but didn't engage us.

"How's your hand?" Matthew asked.

I flexed my left hand through the gauze and tape, which I'd had to reapply several times since being treated by the guy in the infirmary. "Fine," I said. "I've had worse."

"Do you have a break soon?" Matthew asked, leaning in closer.

I inched onto the counter—like Candace was always being reprimanded for—so I could be those few inches closer to him. "My shift just started. I don't usually get to sit down until the sun goes down."

"You're sitting right now." He smirked.

"You know what I mean." I scooted even closer to him, as far as the prep counter would allow, and leaned against the bar. "What is that?" I asked, grabbing hold of his left hand and twisting it so I could see the full image of his tattoo.

Matthew tensed under my touch, but didn't pull his hand back. Instead, he sucked in an anxious breath before speaking. "The official symbol of the Society. The same thing you have on your necklace."

"It's beautiful," I said, tracing the intricate lines

with my forefinger—lines I could feel like raised black scars on his flesh. My cheek burned at the thought.

"You'll get one when you're initiated," he said, his voice soft to keep the conversation private between us.

The thought of getting a large tattoo like his made me lightheaded. I couldn't even make it through a cut on the hand. How could I get through the needlework to have that elaborate picture drawn on my skin?

"Don't worry; you'll be fine," he said, as if reading my mind. "I'll be with you." And my inquisitive look convinced him to add, "You're biting your lip. There are plenty of things to be nervous about, but this shouldn't be one of them."

"That's cool," Alexis said, now standing next to me, gazing down at Matthew's tattoo. "Got any more?"

"No; just the one."

When I glanced toward the espresso bar to see how Candace was faring, I saw her put the last of the drinks on the bar. Mallory left without another word, her loquacious friends in tow.

"That was amazing," Candace said, joining us on the opposite side of the register. "What did you do to her? I've never seen Mallory so... so accommodating."

"I don't know what you're talking about," Matthew said, slyly.

"Well, whatever it was, I like having you around. You should be here like all the time."

"Thanks," Matthew said.

"Have you girls even moved since I left?" Eli said, strolling back onto the floor, still tying his apron.

"We helped at least a hundred customers," Alexis said.

"As well as the Queen Bee herself," Candace added. "She even let me make her drink."

"Wow… I didn't think I'd ever see the day," Eli said, sounding genuinely impressed.

"I know. Right?"

"Okay; Candace, you've earned your ten. Get out of here."

"Already gone."

More customers entered the store just in time for Candace to weasel past them and out the door. I knew I'd be heading to the espresso bar with her gone.

"Are you gonna hang out for a while?" I asked, taking Matthew's now empty mug.

"I better let you get back to work," he said, stepping off his stool. "I just wanted to see you in your environment for once. And I should also tell you that your first training session is tomorrow night. I'll pick you up at eight."

"I work tomorrow night."

"Then you'll have to get your shift covered," he said, matter-of-factly.

I shook my head with a frown. I hadn't heard from him in over three days and now he was telling me I needed to change my work schedule with less than a day's notice? "Thanks for the warning," I said.

"Fiona, you've got drinks piling up over here," Eli said.

"I'm coming!" I called.

"I know you'll be able to handle it," Matthew said, flashing me one of his brilliant smiles. His teeth were perfect—straight and proportionate.

"I'll work something out," I said, my smile certainly not on par with his. I ran a hand through my hair, unconsciously straightening it over my right cheek.

"I'll see you at eight."

Matthew's penetrating gaze remained fixed on me for a long moment, reminding me of the night in his SUV. A part of me wanted to rush around the counter and wrap my arms around his neck, but knew how silly that sounded. In reality, I couldn't move—even though Eli was still calling for me to help out.

It was almost painful when our connection broke. However, it was also undeniably agonizing to watch him leave.

19

MATTHEW

J didn't think much of Catherine anymore. She was my maker—the vampire who turned me. Dr. Catherine Mercer had been a staff member at Sisters of Mercy when I'd been institutionalized by Frederick. And she was the only woman I had allowed myself to fully love.

Her love for me convinced her to turn me without my consent. At that time, I hadn't thought of her in such affectionate terms. She'd always been good and gentle with me, but I still viewed her as one of those monsters—an evil bloodsucker like all the rest. They were heartless, soulless fiends who didn't know the meaning of the word *love*. But my prejudices changed when I became one of them.

It wasn't until she turned me that I fully understood and appreciated how she'd been trying to save me. It wasn't until then that I saw the full vision for my future and what I had really been brought there to do. It wasn't until shortly after my turning that I'd begun to return the affection Catherine had for me—until it was mutual love and admiration. She was a beautiful creature of the night who struggled with what she'd become, a struggle I also felt every day. But Frederick punished me for that love and ripped her away from me, determined to keep me from the ones I loved until I succumbed to his will and gave him the proof he craved. But I vowed never to let him witness the truth for himself, the proof I coveted and built the True North Society around.

I took Catherine's last name after she was taken from me, so that a part of her could live, and that same part of me could be forgotten forever. Over the next few decades, I tried several more relationships, but they all found violent ends, even with careful measures taken to conceal them. Frederick was always watching. He never forgave Catherine for depriving him of his frail, human toy, and never forgave me for taking over Sisters of Mercy less than a decade later. As time went by, the people around us died, but our resentments remained.

But through it all, Frederick had no intention of killing me, even with my numerous attempts on his life. This was his game—our dance.

And now I had Fiona, the most important person in my life since Catherine, and I couldn't let Frederick get to her. I couldn't show him how much she meant to me—how important she was.

I had to keep my distance. There was no other choice. Even though I hadn't coached a candidate since Ashley nearly half a century earlier, it didn't have to be obvious to those looking in that Fiona was significant to me.

I warmed up a packet of animal blood in the microwave, then cut it open and poured the contents into a glass. Going from Taylor's blood to this wasn't fulfilling, but I had to get back into the habit— recondition my distinguished taste. I equated animal blood to water. It did the job it was supposed to do— no more, no less. Well, maybe sometimes less. On the other hand, human blood was more like drinking the finest wine and getting the perfect buzz without the hangover. All I had to do was live with the guilt, which many of my kind no longer felt—though not all.

I downed the glass in one long gulp, then heated up a second packet, knowing I couldn't pick up Fiona tonight with even a half-empty stomach. While I sipped from the second glass, I peered out of a living room window from my top floor apartment, admiring the lit landscape of artificial light through the bleak metal bars as the last rays of sunlight dipped beneath the Pacific Ocean. A radiant cluster of lights off to the northwest was Los Angeles in all its deceptive glory.

The monsters were always out, but after sundown, they were out en masse, more apt to show their true colors. And there were places they could do so more safely—like Sisters of Mercy for one, not far from here, and Fangloria for another, in the underbelly of the city. There were smaller, less well-known establishments hidden in plain sight, rising and falling on a regular basis—a part of the Vampire Nation movement. We knew they were signaling the beginning of the end.

The beginning of the end.

I took the final sip from my glass and retreated from the window. I rinsed the glass and placed it into the dishwasher. Most of the other residents who lived on the upper floors of the penitentiary had daily maid service like a five-star hotel, but I was the only vampire permanently residing in the building. I had enough regular human interactions; I didn't need one more—especially within my personal space.

Now that I'd gotten Taylor kicked out of the building—out of her onsite residence—I could rest a little bit easier. I'd never pursued her, but she'd become obsessed. I'd still have to occasionally run into her within Society work and events, but at least my home was now off limits. And if it was discovered she'd been branded with Vampire Nation—as many vampire groupies tend to do—then she'd be terminated. Problem solved.

I could have baited her and let Frederick take care of her for me, I thought. I'd only have to answer to my own conscience. I'd done worse when I was younger, but tried like hell to be a better man now. The unyielding need for feeding didn't make that easy, and curbing it with animal blood greatly compounded those challenges.

I gazed down at the True North compass on my arm—a constant source of pain—and ran my finger along the tender skin, the one part of me that never healed. The arrow always pointed north, and north was always directed at me.

I recalled Fiona's touch on my arm the night before, her fingers brushing the sensitive flesh I was retracing. It burned with an agony and excitement that scared me even now. I couldn't allow her in—to get too close and tempt fate with what I knew to be true. There was a greater power at work. Our time together was short.

20

FIONA

*M*atthew picked me up in a parking lot near Hot Coffee, so I wouldn't have to explain to Mom where I was going—and who was accompanying me for my evening excursion. I couldn't be seen at Hot Coffee since Candace had agreed to cover my shift, though she'd taken some convincing. I felt I was living a new double life.

Matthew took me to the same building as before, behind the fence and guise of Silverado State Prison. I was given the opportunity to change into some fitness gear in a locker room, offering an assigned locker equipped with True North-supplied exercise gear. The tee shirt even had the now familiar compass emblem on the right breast. I had a pretty good idea these clothes would somehow fit perfectly.

Zelda was just finishing changing when I got to

my locker. To my relief, Mallory wasn't there. When I met up with Matthew in the hallway, he had changed into workout clothes as well—a black sleeveless tee and tight shorts that bulged from his muscular quads. I tried not to look too closely.

"Ready to sweat?" he asked with a sly smile. "You'll probably want to put your hair up."

I had my hair tie around my wrist, but wasn't about to put my hair up unless absolutely necessary. The scar on my cheek burned at the thought of full exposure. At least my shirt wasn't sleeveless.

"I put myself in your capable hands," I finally said, sounding awkward and no longer connected to his statement.

"You won't be at my mercy," he answered as we continued down the hallway.

Matthew led me to a large gymnasium on the same level as the locker rooms. It was currently being used by a number of groups, all sectioned to separate spaces within the oversized room, participating in an eclectic assortment of strength and combat training.

We met the other candidates and coaches in an available corner. I said hi to Zelda and Barry but kept my distance from Mallory as she talked with her coach, ignoring me completely.

After a few minutes of milling about, we were introduced to our trainers, Octavius and Vladimir. We were given protective jackets, masks, and practice sabres—then partnered up to attempt the techniques they'd demonstrated. And we were not paired up with our coaches. Zelda was paired with Barry, leaving me—of course—with the delightful Mallory.

As much as I never wanted to be partnered with her for anything, the thought of sticking her with a fencing sabre sounded pretty good. She didn't say anything as I took a few practice swings, but simply readied her stance.

If only I could really stab you with this thing, I thought, grinning mischievously beneath my mask as we waited for the official notice to proceed with the sparring match.

Once Octavius blew the whistle, metal blades clanged and crashed as the parries between our two pairs began. It didn't take me more than a few seconds to realize Mallory knew exactly what she was doing. She expertly evaded my attacks and swiftly disarmed me of my weapon, sending the sabre skidding across the floor. Her coach, Aaron, stopped it with his foot. He handed it back to me, not even trying to suppress the huge grin on his face. Matthew tried to look more sympathetic.

Shortly after we began again, I found myself on my back, with the button tip of Mallory's blade at my chest.

"Dead," she said through her metal-mesh mask.

Fury raged inside me as we sparred again and again, and each time I was bested in seconds—

finding myself either on the floor or stripped of my weapon. We didn't have to wait for subsequent whistle blows since our sessions kept ending so fast. And each time, she made a dramatic point of killing me off.

Dead. Dead. Dead!

"You look like you could use a break," Mallory said as I brought up my sword to begin a new round. I could sense her sinister sneer from behind her mask.

My back was sore from hitting the mat so many times, and my arm was sore from swinging the sabre. And my chest—well, that was sore too, where she kept poking me to signal herself the victor, even despite the protective coat.

Matthew took me aside several times to provide pointers, but they didn't help. I was just as outmatched at every turn.

"Hopefully, for your sake, this isn't on the final exam," Mallory said, flipping my sabre in the air with the flick of her blade and catching it with ease. "Or maybe I hope it *is* since you don't belong here." The last statement was spoken softer, to keep her superior opinion out of earshot from everyone else.

"I'll be ready, if it is," I promised, then I was on my back again, the button of her sabre digging into my chest.

"No; you won't." Mallory pulled back her blade and knelt beside me, so our masked faces were only inches apart. "I've been preparing for this my whole life. You're a lost little lamb about to be slaughtered. You have no idea what you're up against." She stood up, but didn't offer me a hand, then added, "Always go for the heart. You. Are. Dead."

When I got to my feet, I didn't bother picking up my sabre, signaling I was done—done being beaten and done being tormented. My ego hurt as much as my body, maybe more. And it was infinitely worse that I'd been so severely outmatched by Mallory Fiennes. It seemed she had it better than me in every way. I removed my mask and let it drop to the floor as well. Sweat was pouring down my face and my unbridled hair clung to my cheeks. When I glanced over at Matthew, I saw him cross-armed with a glare that looked positively murderous.

Mallory removed her mask and held it under one arm. "I take it you yield?"

"I'm taking the break you so considerately said I needed," I said, folding my arms and taking a moment to calm my breathing.

Looking around the room, I saw it had significantly cleared out in the past twenty minutes or so, the noise echoing off the high ceiling greatly reduced. Mallory walked off the mat to stand by her coach, but I remained where I was to watch Zelda and Barry continuing to spar. Barry seemed to be winning a majority of the time, but the two were far more evenly matched than Mallory and I were. And with them being evenly matched, it simply meant everyone in the room could kick my ass.

"You did fine for your first session," Matthew said, coming up to stand beside me.

"You don't have to do that," I said in a sulking tone.

"Do what? I didn't say you did well." He gave a half-smile that seemed to suggest he wasn't completely disappointed by my amateur performance.

"Did you know she's been training?"

Matthew nodded. "But I didn't know how proficient she was." He paused while we watched the other candidates compete, then said, "You should look at this as a good thing. She challenges you, which will only make you better, stronger, and faster."

"Yeah; she challenges me every day not to strangle her."

"At this point, I don't think you could." He sounded serious.

I gave him an exaggerated glare of offense and disgust, even though I knew he was right.

"Now, in the spirit of challenging you, I must warn you that the next demonstration is going to seem unbelievable and really screw with your mind. But it's one of the primary reasons you're here. Keep an open mind."

I was about to ask what he was talking about,

when Octavius and Vladimir spoke up to get everyone's attention and announce the next order of business. I suddenly noticed the room had gone deathly quiet, and the other remaining groups of people had stopped what they were doing and were coming over to our little corner of the gymnasium.

"The True North Society covets a number of secrets only hinted at during your initial ceremonies," Octavius said, primarily addressing us four. "One of them you're about to learn right now and it will fundamentally change your perspective of the world. Much of what the Society has to offer is overwhelming and today's demonstration will be no exception. This is why senior members, trainers, and your coaches will only reveal a piece at a time, so the chance for emotional and mental meltdown are adequately anticipated and reduced. Some things are better shown than described, so watch, listen, and learn. There'll be time afterwards for comments and questions."

By this time, Vladimir had his shirt off and was holding an intimidating six-inch dagger in each hand. They looked sharp and deadly, and he looked no less formidable with his large muscles rippling across his entire upper body.

Matthew was now stepping away from me and pulling his shirt up over his head. He was leaner, less bulky than Vladimir, but looked just as rock-solid with perfectly smooth milky white skin. The compass on his forearm truly was his only tattoo. The rest of his skin was flawless and unmarked, so perfectly toned and proportioned that he didn't seem real. I flushed at the thought of his perfection, growing even hotter with the thought of all my scars. Physically he was a better match for Mallory— a thought that made me livid.

Vladimir passed Matthew one of the daggers and they walked out onto a neighboring mat, further away from the gathered crowd of onlookers. Matthew glanced back at me, giving that sad look I'd now seen from him several times and couldn't imagine what was going through his mind—then he opened his mouth wide and growled like an animal —a predator—like the king of the beasts. And as he did so, fangs protruded where his canine teeth had previously been, and I finally saw him for who he truly was.

No...

Matthew jerked the arm holding the dagger and it elongated like a bladed collapsible baton, transforming into a gleaming sword.

Vladimir did the same with his dagger, the metal whining from the friction as it unfolded. Just when I was about to look for his fangs, white feathered wings exploded from his back in a radiant burst of energy.

I was looking upon not one, but two mythical creatures that should not exist outside a movie screen or the pages of a fantastical novel. I hadn't been given any drugs, unless they were pumping them in through the ventilation system. Just like standing on the station in space, looking down at Earth, this seemed to really be happening.

I glanced over at Mallory and found she hadn't been any more prepared for this than I'd been. And if I hadn't been so horrified, I would've taken some joy in that.

The deafening clash of metal brought my attention back to the supernatural beings twenty feet away, engaging each other in an epic battle I could barely comprehend. They moved so fast their bodies began to blur. Their strikes had the power of cars colliding. Vladimir didn't have to stay on the ground, intermittently using his wings to soar around Matthew. But Matthew was not at a disadvantage—his leaps could reach Vladimir at any height within the room.

How is he a vampire...?

I'd seen him outside—in sunlight. He drank coffee. His skin was warm when I'd run my hand down his arm with the tattoo. He'd been nothing but nice to me—despite the whole kidnapping thing, and drugging my friends. This couldn't be the same man.

I watched horrified—mystified—as they brutally attacked each other, then realized... this was what we were training for... not to fight other people, but to defend ourselves from these otherworldly beings.

I was about to use the word *creatures*, but as horrified as I was, they were so absolutely beautiful.

Then Matthew drew first blood, his gleaming blade slicing across Vladimir's right arm. A gruesome crimson arc trailed the tip of the blade, painting the dark mat. The angel took to the air again to get some space, blood pouring down his arm from the deep gash. But the wound didn't seem to be slowing him. A moment later, he was attacking again, and after a few more strikes, speared Matthew through the left shoulder, the end of the blade protruding from his back, red and dripping.

I let out an audible gasp, a hand flying up to my mouth. I began to feel dizzy as tiny stars popped in my periphery.

Vladimir ripped the blade from Matthew's body, and Matthew fell to his knees. Matthew's once beautiful chest was now covered in blood.

I was burning up and finding it hard to breathe. I couldn't watch this. Before I dropped to the mat, I turned and raced out of the gymnasium. Someone yelled my name, but if I stopped and allowed the adrenaline to fall, then so would I—like a rock.

My first victory was making it out into the hallway. I rounded several corners before stopping, finding myself alone in this deceptive building, filled with deceptive people, a part of a deceptive world I didn't understand anymore. Even though I regularly spoke with my deceased sister, I thought I had this world all figured out—thought I knew what was real and what wasn't, what was possible and what was impossible.

I couldn't catch my breath as I fell against the wall and sank to the floor. Everything hit me all at once. Big uncontrollable sobs overtook me as I hugged my knees, wishing I was back at home, safe in the confines of my room with my sister looking over me. All I had wanted to do was find my father. It was the only reason I had signed up for this crazy adventure. But now... It was no longer a crazy adventure, but a nightmare.

I wiped the tears from my eyes to bring the world back into focus, to make sure someone wasn't sneaking up on me from either end of the hallway. Then my paranoia brought my attention upward like some creature could be stalking me from the ceiling. I had no idea what was impossible now.

I was still alone in the hallway. Across from me was a closed door. I thought I could read the nameplate on it, but my lingering tears blurred the letters from this distance. Wiping my eyes again, I pushed up to my feet and took the few steps to the door, my eyes glued to the nameplate. As I drew closer, it all came into focus—everything—confirming my original suspicions.

Roland Damascus.

My father.

FIONA

J think my body shook more from seeing my father's name on the door than from the revelation of the mythical beings in the gymnasium. My tears dried up immediately from the combination of curiosity, longing, and rage. They couldn't deny me some answers now. My search had led me here, and this was the door standing between me and my lifelong questions.

"Fiona," a voice called from down the hallway.

I turned to see Matthew standing at the far intersection, still shirtless—a navy blue towel in his hand, wiping residual blood from his upper body, turning the towel nearly purple. It was obvious now that he didn't have a scratch on him; whatever wounds had been inflicted during the fight were completely healed. His beautiful skin was flawless once again.

When he saw the troubled look on my face and

realized the location of where I was standing, he didn't bother saying anything else, but raced to my side.

"I'm sorry," he said, so close I could feel his breath on my face. He smelled as sweet as ever, no hint of sweat even after all the exertion put forth in the demonstration. Then again, perhaps he didn't have to exert himself at all. "I know that was a lot to take in."

I backed up a step, still envisioning the vicious fangs protruding from his gums and the demonic look in his eyes when he attacked. I didn't know what to make of him now... now that I knew what he was truly capable of.

"I know you're afraid," he said softy, his words as soothing as a lullaby. "Rightly so. You have a lot to be afraid of in this world. But we will give you the tools to conquer that fear and fight back. I may be a monster, but I'm not evil. I don't take pleasure in other people's pain."

"What about my father?" I asked, pointing to the nameplate. "Is he one of you—a vampire?"

"No," Matthew said. "I am one of the few vampires in the Society. You'll come to discover that most of the people here despise vampires, and for good reason. I deal with the condemnation in a place where I can attempt to do the most good."

I reached for the door handle, finding it locked.

"Don't," he said. "You've been shown enough for

one night. I want to help you process what you've seen. I'll answer the initial questions you have for me."

"You can't deny me this time," I insisted, tugging at the doorknob to show my insistence and defiance.

Matthew placed a hand over mine, causing me to flinch and try to pull away, but he denied me that reprieve. His hand held me in place while I slowly accepted and gave in to his touch.

"I need to know you're okay."

"I'm so very *not* okay," I retorted, almost laughing as I said it while tears once again brimmed in my eyes.

"Promise me you can handle this and not go running off again," Matthew clarified.

I didn't know how I could honestly promise such a thing, but I did what I needed to do to get through this door. "I promise."

"Then stay right here," Matthew instructed and disappeared in a flash, once again demonstrating the speed shown in the fight with Vladimir. Before I even had a chance to wonder how long he'd be gone, Matthew rounded the corner at lightning speed, now without the towel and holding this tee shirt in one hand and a small card in the other. He took the card and swiped it along the keypad next to the door until the light flashed green.

Matthew held open the door and flipped on the lights, allowing me to walk into what looked like an office. My legs trembled as I stepped into the room. Since the lights had been off, I didn't expect to find anyone inside, but the mere thought of entering a room that belonged to my father—that housed some of my father's belongings—was still utterly terrifying, so much so that the idea of entering a confined room with a vampire didn't even cross my mind.

This room didn't look much different from the one in which I'd changed into the red dress before the branding ceremony. There was an oversized desk, a wall of bookcases, a leather couch and a few matching chairs, an en-suite bathroom, and framed pictures on the wall spouting clichéd inspirational quotes. The air was musty, like the door hadn't been opened in quite some time. A light film of dust covered the desk; it also held a stack of papers, but no computer that I could see.

Stepping up to the desk, I picked up a small framed picture. It showed the smiling face of a little girl with long brunette hair, pinned back from her face with a purple barrette. She looked like me, but it was a picture I'd never seen before. There was no scar on the girl's face, so if it truly was me, then it was taken before my attack. And if the picture was from before the attack, then Becca would still have been alive.

"Who is this?" I asked, accusatorily.

"Her name is Abigail," Matthew said, now fully clothed, taking the picture frame from me to examine it closer. Instead of handing it back to me, he set the frame back on the table exactly where the dust dictated.

"Is she his daughter?" I asked, my throat closing up as I struggled to get the words out.

Matthew nodded, stepping back to give me more room to breathe.

"Does he even know about me… and Rebecca?" These words were even harder to get out.

"Yes; he knew about both of you," he said solemnly, and it didn't get by me that he used the past tense, but I didn't press it in that moment.

I stepped behind the desk and sat down on the oversized leather chair, thrown a little by how much it rocked. The office looked and felt like a tomb, every item in it seemingly undisturbed for months. I'd hoped I could get a real sense of him from being in this room, but I didn't. Settling my attention on the ajar door to the en-suite, I got up and wandered over to the bathroom. It was stocked with the basics, but nothing that made it look lived in. There was nothing specifically of my father's in here besides the picture.

"He hasn't been in here in a long time," I said.

"No."

"What's this office for? What does he do for you?"

"Do you remember your first night with us—on the space station?"

"Was I really on a space station?"

"As real as anything else you've ever stepped inside."

"How was that possible?"

Matthew shook his head. "I can't go into the specifics now. But you do remember the station?"

"Yes," I said, impatiently.

"Your father was the chief designer of that," Matthew said. "He was a key member of our operation."

There it was—Matthew using the past tense again, like my father was gone or dead. Every revelation seemed to lead to a million more questions, quickly coaxing my head to explode.

"So, where is he?" I finally asked—addressing the real elephant in the room. "I want you to take me to him."

"Now, that's something I can't do at this time." Matthew looked genuinely apologetic, but he did not waver in his resolve.

"I don't accept that," I said, holding my ground.

"Well, you must, *candidate*," Matthew said, stepping closer to me.

His imposing presence and the transformation I'd seen before caused me to back away from him again. I was powerless here and we both knew it. As much as I wanted to stand and be strong, I wasn't. I was only here because I couldn't handle what had been happening in the gymnasium. I was the weak link in this new group of candidates, having run off like a scared little girl. They'd label me as such going forward. Mallory certainly wouldn't miss an opportunity to give me more hell. I didn't want to go back and face everyone. I just wanted to go home.

"You've gotten a glimpse into your father's life, which was more than you were supposed to get until after you were initiated. I know how important this is to you, so I felt it necessary to extend some goodwill. Come back to the gymnasium. Ask some questions or simply listen and be part of the team."

"I can't go back," I said.

"Ever?"

"I don't know, but certainly not right now." I said, sniffling—trying to prevent more tears from falling. "Just give me one more straight answer. Will I get to meet him?"

Matthew nodded. "You will." He paused, his eyes trying to read mine. "So, what now?"

"I want to go home... now."

"Can I take you?"

At first, his question threw me off guard. Then I considered what his question truly meant. Did I still trust him... Well, did I? I needed to ask a bunch of questions around what a real vampire was. Where did real vampires fit in the natural order of things? What were they really capable of? I assumed the demonstration was just the tip of the iceberg. As leery as I was, if Matthew's intention was to harm me, he would have done so already. He'd had ample opportunities. I certainly didn't consider myself safe, but safe enough for the moment.

"You may," I said, biting my lip, still nervous of the position I was in.

"Then go change," he said. "I'll take you home right away. I'll give you time to process, but won't allow you to quit."

Since this enigmatic place held the secret of my father, I had to battle my fears and continue my training. I couldn't allow myself to quit either, no matter how much I wanted to right now. The silver lining was that he seemed to have some degree of confidence in me.

MATTHEW

The drive home with Fiona was silent and tense. She could have asked any number of questions about what she had seen, but she didn't ask a single one. In fact, she barely looked at me throughout the entire ride. When she exited the Land Rover, she said *goodnight* but gave me a melancholy look, like we were parting ways for good. Of course, I wouldn't let that happen, but her internal conflict was clear.

Even though this new distance between us was a good thing for Fiona, I couldn't help but feel saddened by it. It was frustrating being so drawn to her. I just had to keep reminding myself that her apprehension toward me—now that she saw me for me—was a good thing.

I drove straight back to headquarters, knowing I had to update the Assembly of Seven with the status and progress of my candidate. And Fiona certainly wasn't favored amongst the other candidates.

I bumped into Aaron on my way to the conference room, Mallory still with him, as smug as ever.

"Has your candidate quit yet?" Aaron asked. "She sure ran out of the gym fast when she discovered what you were. You should have known better than to insist on being a coach."

"She's not going to quit," I insisted, trying my best to keep from knocking his head off his shoulders. He was a well-trained fighter from the Society's perspective, but he obviously needed the tools —the toys the Society provided—to do any damage to me.

"Give her time." Aaron laughed, glancing over at Mallory, who simply gave an amused smile. "Fencing obviously isn't her thing. She can't handle a little blood. It's well known she has daddy issues. You have to admit, she's not cut out for this. Everyone here knows it."

"She'll surprise you—all of you. Just watch." I walked off before the urge became too great to keep from picking him up by the neck and slamming his insignificant body against the wall.

I heard Aaron call out from behind me, "We'll see." Then I tuned them out completely. I didn't want to tap into their conversation as we drew further away from each other and they didn't think I could hear them anymore. The fact that I could hear so much better than a human was a blessing and a curse.

I continued toward the third-floor conference room, where I knew the Assembly of Seven would be waiting. These seven members made up our elite council. Anderson was just finishing up his report on Zelda when I arrived.

As soon as he finished up, I was allowed in. "All yours," Anderson said as he passed me to exit the room. Anderson closed the door behind him.

"Please take a seat," President Bolt said, sitting at the far head of the oblong table. She was flanked by three assemblymen on each side.

I claimed the one empty leather seat closest to the door. I knew exactly who wanted me to be here and who didn't. I'd watched this entire council turn over throughout the years. I'd appointed the first assemblymen to this council, though I'd never appointed myself to one of the open seats. After that, my influence on successors waned. Now, there were only two assemblymen who actively wanted me here, two who continued to see my value but remained neutral, and the assemblymen who detested my involvement in any official capacity— the most vocal of whom was Assemblyman Douglas Fiennes.

"It seems Roland's daughter is having difficulties," President Bolt said. She was a tall and thick woman with graying hair, which she didn't try to conceal.

She had been on the assembly for three decades, being elected President twelve years earlier. And we all knew there wouldn't be another election and that she'd guide us into our final days.

"And that's as most of us foresaw," Douglas added. He was Mallory's father and my biggest critic, now on the assembly nearly a decade. He'd been appointed when Roland Damascus was relieved of his seat. Assemblyman Fiennes looked like he should be a vampire with his larger-than-life wiry build, tight skin, and permanent scowl. But he detested supernatural beings in all their forms—vampires and angels alike—and pushed to get bylaws passed for us to be removed from the society permanently. So far, that hadn't passed with a majority vote, but our access and membership was limited.

"It is true, Fiona's had some difficulties, but nothing she won't be able to overcome," I said. "The car accident she was in before the pledging offer was made shook her up, so she's had to deal with a lot in a short period."

"You can't blame her reaction tonight on a car accident," Douglas said with a laugh.

"I'm not," I said, glaring at him. "I'm simply framing her fragile behavior as of late."

"We shouldn't be taking in fragile people at all. We need true fighters for the cause."

"She was guaranteed an opportunity," Assembly-woman Ashley Degray said. She was a tough woman, now in her early seventies. She'd kept healthy and fit throughout the years, never letting her age slow her down. She was the one other candidate I'd officially coached over fifty years earlier. The difference was that she knew about me—about what I was—before being given the pledge. I'd helped her reach the Assembly of Seven at a time when I carried more influence, and she'd since kept me from losing too much more ground with the ever-changing management of the Society.

"We promised Damascus ten years ago, when he was pushed out of the Assembly, but that's not something we need to honor now," Douglas said.

"And who led the charge in pushing him out of the Assembly?" I asked.

"I don't know what you're insinuating since I wasn't on the Assembly at the time. You're supposed to have a far superior memory to us, so I'd think you'd at least remember that."

"I remember a great deal," I spat. "I remember building this society and what life was like for us before. No one in this room has that firsthand knowledge but me. Damascus sacrificed his life for our cause. The least we can do is honor our original promise."

"I didn't make that pr—"

"Quiet, Douglas," President Bolt said, raising a hand. "That original promise is the reason she is here. But the promise did not give her—or anyone for that matter—a guaranteed spot within the Society, let alone a spot on the station."

"This is the final candidate class," Ashley said. "We have more than four spots that have not been sold yet. And we've secured spots for every direct member so far. Our final members should not be denied that privilege now."

"Why is this even up for contention?" Assemblyman Bruce Roselli asked. He was a medium-built man in his fifties with rounded features, a bulbous nose, and thinning salt-and-pepper hair. He was one of the proud-to-be neutrals who didn't want to make too many waves and simply live the rest of his days in the security the True North Society provided. "We have the census. We know who will be aboard and who won't."

"And we know who will be initiated and who won't," Assemblywoman Degray added.

"The census and the logs are incomplete. Matthew knows that better than anyone. But with what records we do have, they shouldn't stop us from doing our due diligence. The records should simply provide a backcheck that we are on track," President Bolt said.

"And we *are* on track," I said confidently. "Fiona has had a rough start; I do not deny that. But that does not mean she will not be a good candidate and asset in the years to come. Some of our best initiates have had similar initial setbacks."

"What are you going to do differently going forward, to ensure her progress?"

"I can now use myself as that training advantage," I said. "Now that she's getting over the initial shock, we can progress leaps and bounds above the rest of the candidate class."

"Wishful thinking," Douglas scoffed. "My daughter has been unknowingly training for years, for which she'll now finally receive acknowledgement. Fiona will not be able to make up for that in just a few weeks. Her body's fragile and her mind is fragile too; we're simply wasting our resources on a girl we should have never extended an invitation to in the first place."

"Fiona's not as fragile as you all might think," I said. "I implore you to allow me to continue her training—give her a fighting chance. She'll be as ready as the others."

"Doubtful. Very doubtful."

"She may even save *your* daughter one day."

"I hope I'm around to see that," Douglas laughed.

FIONA

The door to my room crashed open as Mom rushed in like she was going to kill someone—like I was under attack. She found me in bed, gripping the covers for dear life, drenched in cold sweat.

Mom stopped and surveyed the room, finding everything in order. She let out a long breath before asking, "Are you all right?"

I could still hear my screams echoing in my head, not initially realizing at least some of them had also been aloud. Nodding weakly, I loosened my grip on my covers, only to find the portion of the sheet where my left hand had been balled up was covered in blood. Mom noticed the blood as soon as I did.

She sat on the edge of the bed and took my injured hand in hers. Where the cut was healing from the branding ceremony, I'd reopened part of the wound with my nails from squeezing so hard. She unraveled the stained gauze on my hand and found I'd split one of the butterfly band-aids and one of my nails had dug right into the scabbing cut. It continued to bleed and just looking at it was making me queasy.

"Let me fix you up," Mom insisted and led me to the bathroom, where she redid my bandages with speed and precision. I'd forgotten how capable she was with basic first aid since I usually tried to take care of my own injuries personally. "This is a pretty good cut. You should probably have gotten stitches."

"It'll be fine," I said.

"Just keep it clean and closed." She placed the excess items under the sink, then stood up and eyed me wearily. "Are you okay to go back to sleep? You can come sleep with me, if you want."

"I'm fine, Mom," I said. "But thank you."

"Do you want to talk about your dream?"

"I—I wish I remembered it," I lied.

"Okay," she said and kissed my forehead. "Stop scaring me, kid."

"I'm trying," I said, forcing a small smile.

We both went back to our respective rooms. I quickly changed the bedsheets, placing the bloody ones in a pile next to my hamper. Before climbing into bed, I peeked out the window at the still dark parking lot. It was almost 4 a.m. and all was quiet, then I noticed a shadowy coyote jogging between the parked cars. I hadn't seen one around here in years, and now I'd seen two in the past month. At least this one seemed less out of place, hunting at night.

I called to my sister as I tucked myself in, before turning out the light.

"I'm here, Fee," Becca said. "Are you okay?"

"Yeah; just a nightmare," I said. "I just wanted to make sure you were here." Feeling a little safer, I turned off the light and shut my eyes, trying to think of anything other than the monsters I now knew lurked in the dark.

THE NEXT NIGHT, I woke up in a similar cold sweat, but there was no blood this time, and Mom didn't come crashing into my room with a baseball bat. I must have kept my nightmare to myself this time. However, my sheets were soaked and I hadn't washed the bloody set yet, so I had to just deal with it. I threw off the comforter, which helped a little, but it was still hard to get back to sleep.

"Another bad dream?" Becca asked.

"How could you tell?" I asked, sarcastically.

"You were moving a lot and mumbling. I don't know what you were saying."

"I don't either, but yeah—another nightmare." I could still picture the vampires attacking me. Everyone I knew had been turned into them—into horrible creatures—all of them after me. Matthew had unleashed them all on me. They were surrounding me, fangs bared and glistening, ready to tear me apart and suck me dry, not something I wanted to reenact or try to explain to a six-year-old or even the ghost of one.

"Night, night," Becca said. "See you in the morning, in the morning."

"Night, night," I repeated like a sweet nursery rhyme. "See you in the morning, in the morning."

On NIGHT THREE, Mòm came rushing in again. This time, I was outside my covers and crying uncontrollably.

"What's going on?" Mom asked, sitting beside me on the bed. "Something's got you freaked out. School? Work? Friends? College apps? What is it?"

I couldn't tell her what was really causing the nightmares, but I could give her a nugget of my insecurities. "Everything's changing," I said, wiping my nose and eyes on the back of my non-bandaged hand.

"That's what happens as you grow older," she said in a soothing voice. "The world changes. The people around you change. *You* change. It's the one constant in life. You can fight it, but you can't stop it. It's much more beneficial to learn to embrace it."

"But I want things to stay the way they are —*were*."

"I know, kiddo." She rubbed my back as I lay on my side to face her. "And I wanted you and your sister to remain six forever, back when I felt like I had control and could keep you safe. I know better now—even though I can't stop trying. And I know I have to let you go out into the world and pave your own path. As scary as it is for you, just remember it's as equally scary for me. No matter how old you get, you'll always be my little girl."

"Enough with the cheesy parenting lines," I laughed, my breathing finally normalizing.

Before she left, Mom kissed my forehead and tucked me back under the covers like she'd done when I was young—like she'd always done with Rebecca and me when we'd shared this room, her bed once where my desk now stood against the wall.

"I don't like seeing you like this," Becca said, her voice always music to my ears.

"I'll be okay," I said. I knew I would be, just as soon as I was fully able to accept and embrace my new life—the new world I'd been introduced to. I'd gone eighteen years without being attacked by a vampire, so what made me so afraid I'd suddenly be attacked now? They were either experts at hiding in plain sight or there weren't many around. I hoped for the latter, but already knew how well they could blend in from my time spent with Matthew.

I still didn't know how to feel about him. He'd been all I could think about since the first day I met him, but now it was for very different reasons. I couldn't help being terrified of him now. I didn't know how I could continue training with him, but couldn't forget my father was in that building some-where—or at least, I assumed he was. I owed it to Becca and myself to know what happened to him. Why had he abandoned us? Why had he never come looking for us—until now?

As afraid as I was, I couldn't quit.

24

MATTHEW

I stopped by Sisters of Mercy at the height of visiting hours, when the hospital was really alive. It was quarter past 1 a.m. when I entered and greeted the reception nurse. I'd seen her before, but she was relatively new to the staff and I couldn't remember her name. But she knew exactly who I was.

"Good evening, Mr. Mercer," she said, cheerfully.

"Good evening," I said, nodding to her as I strolled past the reception desk. I used my keycard to enter the patient area and navigated the hallways toward the administration management offices.

The hallways were active with nurses and doctors, VIP guests and patients. As much as we focused on training new and transitioning vampires, we also had to pay the bills to remain independent from the True North Society. Before the focus had become vampire training, it had been on the entertainment and pleasure of wealthy vampire patrons. They paid for uncensored access to our patients during visiting hours. The only limitation was keeping our patients alive. I had endured these horrors firsthand when I'd been committed to this institution, thanks to the facility's original owner, Frederick. When I took over, I wanted to put an end to the barbaric practice, but it was a necessary evil to keep the facility profitable and focused on the greater good.

"I hope I'm not disturbing anything," I said, knocking on Jack's door, noticing Ashley Degray was also present. I was surprised to see her at such an hour, but knew she couldn't stay away from this facility. It had made her into the woman she was today—irreversibly changing her life path. She'd also changed Jack's life forever and had made a major impact on mine as well. He'd started out there as an orderly, as all transitioning born vampires were prescribed to do, and she was one of his patients, having just turned eighteen. This had been in the winter of 1965.

"Not at all, Matthew," Ashley said. "We were just reviewing the current patient roster to see how many rooms needed to be filled, and if any of the current patients can be or are on track for repositioning."

"The assembly doesn't keep you busy enough?" I

said with a chuckle, entering the office and closing the door behind me.

"I still enjoy her company," Jack said. "What can I say? She's a very special woman."

"You don't have to tell me," I said, taking a seat on the opposite side of the desk from the two of them. "She's been fighting for me for years."

"Fiennes has it out for you," Ashley said. "Be careful with him. He's lobbying to get you excommunicated."

"He's been trying ever since he got onto the Assembly. I should have killed him then."

"You can't easily get away with that now."

"Which is why he's still alive," I said, though I had other reasons for keeping him alive that I wasn't willing to disclose to them—even if they were some of my closest friends.

"Can I offer you a drink?" Jack asked.

I raised an eyebrow at him.

"You still off human blood?"

I nodded.

"Good; I've got you covered," he said and rolled his chair to a mini fridge and removed a blood bag. He ripped it open and poured the thick liquid into a glass, placing it into the microwave on top of the fridge.

"I'm so proud of you," Ashley said. "You've come such a long way since I first met you."

"I don't know about that, but I'm trying," I said.

"I don't know how you do it," Jack said and passed me the warm glass. "I've only killed one human in my life, but couldn't function without human blood. I mean, I mix it up, but I couldn't live on animal blood alone."

"Well, you're going to have to once I'm gone," Ashley said with a sarcastic grin. "I won't be around forever."

"I'll just have to freeze your remaining blood and make it last—to get me through the long winter," Jack said, leaning in to kiss her on the cheek.

I'd envied their relationship, which had endured the better part of fifty years, especially with Ashley refusing to be turned. They'd only ever had eyes for each other, even with Ashley growing older every year. Jack looked very similar to the way he'd looked when they'd first met, his aging already having started decelerating, then freezing completely once his transition was complete. Age never seemed to be a factor for them, and he'd remain devoted to her until the day she died. As far as I knew, he'd never strayed—not once in all these years.

I sipped from the glass of blood. "Is this deer blood?" I asked.

"Very good," Jack said. "I shot it myself, hunting with some buddies earlier this season. I took the blood and donated the meat."

"I used to hunt deer years ago—at one time, it

was my meal of choice," I said. "I've been a little too preoccupied lately."

"Which is probably the real reason you're here… unless you're looking to indulge…" Jack gave me a wink, his expression turning sheepish when he noticed Ashley glaring at him.

"*This* is my indulgence for the evening," I said, holding up my half-empty glass. "I wanted to follow up on our new friend from the accident since I hadn't heard anything from you."

"You could have just called," Jack said.

"I couldn't sleep and wanted to see some friendly faces."

"Well, I don't have any updates yet. If I did, I would have called you immediately."

"I figured as much," I said, my shoulders slumping as I downed the rest of the blood. "Is there anything you need from me?"

"No; I've got my feelers out," Jack said. "These things take time, but I'm confident I'll have something soon. If he was sloppy enough to be caught on one video, he's bound to show up somewhere else. We just need to find it."

"Is there something you want the Society doing?" Ashley asked. "I can gather some additional resources."

I shook my head. "I'm keeping this operation outside of the Society. But if you could, just keep an ear out for anything against Fiona."

"You already know there are plenty of people against her."

"But is there anyone actively going after her?"

"Not that I know of, but I'll keep my ears open," Ashley said, taking the empty glass from me and setting it on a side table.

"That's all I ask," I said, thanking them for their help, and taking my leave of Sisters of Mercy.

I'd given Fiona a few days now to adjust to her new paradigm—one where she was living her daily life with monsters of folklore. I knew if I gave her too long, she'd be more resistant to continuing her candidacy. I needed to set up a meeting with her soon to keep her progressing. I thought she'd benefit from some one-on-one instruction, outside of the group training sessions.

I knew it was late but was compelled to reach out while I was thinking about her, so I sent a simple text before heading home. Since it was in the middle of the night, I didn't expect to receive a response until sometime the next day—if at all—but was surprised when my phone lit up while I was leaving the parking lot a few minutes later.

I read the returned message and smiled.

Not a chance.

25

FIONA

Matthew texted me before I had the chance to fall back to sleep. Mom had left my room about fifteen minutes earlier and Becca had been doing her best to comfort me. My mind was still preoccupied with the nightmares and my changing reality, so sleep was doing its best to elude me. Now adding Matthew to the mix just made it that much harder.

I hope you're not considering quitting.

I stared at the message, reading it over and over as I thought of everything I'd been through in the past few weeks, how much my life had really changed. I didn't know if he expected me to be up at that hour, but I didn't want to procrastinate in responding. If I slept on it, who knew what new rationalization would come to me?

Not a chance.

A few minutes later, Matthew responded to my message with a smiley-faced emoji. The little yellow smiling face on my screen made me grin in return; I couldn't deny my intrigue, even though it was now intermingled with fear. Maybe I'd finally be able to get some sleep, and I turned out to be right.

The next morning, I felt more rested than any other day that week. I was able to get ready for school in less of a fog than what had become my new normal. I even got away with cutting out the extra cup of coffee I'd been drinking over the past few days, just to stay awake through my classes.

I'd been catching glances from Mallory several times a day all week, and that day was no different. I couldn't help but think she was keeping an eye on me, maybe providing information back to her coach —thus back to the True North Society—about their black sheep candidate. As if I didn't have enough to be paranoid about, without being on Mallory's spy list.

Alexis drove me to work since our shifts started at the same time. As usual, Candace was already there, starting about two hours earlier. Eli didn't mind if we made our own drinks while there was a lull in customers, and the middle of the afternoon usually provided that lull.

"Are you feeling all right?" Alexis asked, sitting next to me at the bar. She poured another packet of sweetener into her iced tea.

I was slumped forward on my stool, cradling my white mocha with both hands. I'd put an extra shot of espresso in my drink, which also made me add two more pumps of white mocha to counteract the bitterness, making up for the coffee I'd cut out earlier.

"I'm just tired; that's all," I said, then took a careful sip of my drink, which turned out to be more tepid than I'd expected. I frowned at my disappointing beverage, for which I only had myself to blame.

"It's not just today. You haven't seemed yourself all week."

"Just tired," I reiterated. "I haven't been sleeping well." I paused to take another sip. "Have you heard back from any of your colleges yet?"

"A few. I didn't get into UCLA, but we all knew that was a long shot," Alexis said.

"And that's why I decided to spare myself the extra stress," Candace said, walking up to where we were seated. No one was left waiting for a drink and there were only a few customers seated in the lobby.

"By going to JC," Alexis said, rolling her eyes.

"In two years, I'll be able to transfer to UCLA if I so choose," Candace said, stuffing her hands into the pockets of her apron. "Maybe I'll do it just to spite you."

"A valid way of choosing your school of higher education," I said with a laugh.

"Damn right. I'll also be saving like ten grand or more."

"Language," Eli said, passing us to the register. "And how many times do I have to tell you to get your butt off the counter?"

"At least one more," Candace said, hopping down.

Our shift was about to start, so I quickly changed into my work tee shirt in the bathroom, donned my apron, and took over for Candace at the espresso machine as several groups of customers entered the shop together. Candace went on her break and Eli disappeared into the office as usual, leaving Alexis and me to take care of the rush.

About two hours into my shift, I walked over to the register to grab a cup from Alexis, when I noticed Matthew sitting at the bar. A shiver snaked up my spine as our eyes met, and he greeted me with a disarming smile.

"How long have you been here?" I asked—after it took me a moment to find my voice.

"I just sat down," Matthew said.

"I was wondering when you'd come back," Candace said as she came out from the storage room with a few bags of coffee to display in the lobby.

"I couldn't stay away too long," Matthew said, his eyes following Candace as she walked around the bar before returning to me. "You offer the best damn coffee in the county, right?"

"Right," I said, the word catching in my throat.

"Want me to take care of that, so you can talk with your new guy?" Alexis said and snatched the empty cup out of my hand and sauntered over to the espresso station.

"He's not my…" my voice trailed off as I lost the will to fight her comment. "Do you want a coffee?"

"If you're offering," Matthew said, his smile still as radiant as ever, no hint of gruesome fangs.

When I poured his coffee into a warm porcelain mug, I found my hands shaking. I left quite a bit of room at the top, not for him to add creamer, but to keep me from spilling it all over my hands as I carried the steaming mug over to him.

"Do you have a break coming up?" he asked, sliding the mug closer to him and inhaling the earthy aroma before taking a loud sip.

"You can go first," Alexis said to me, as she made her way back to the register. "Have a nice day," she called to the customer headed for the door.

For some reason, I felt safer on the clock with the bar between us—almost as if he couldn't touch me in here. But I knew that was silly. The center was growing pretty busy with dinner time approaching, so no matter where we decided to sit, we wouldn't be alone.

"I'll ask," I finally said.

Eli let me go, so I folded my apron, made another white mocha—no modifications to my regular recipe this time, having learned from my previous disaster—and led Matthew to a table just outside the shop. I made sure we were still in plain view of the rest of the crew, seated at a table positioned next to the glass, on the opposite side of the now decorative roaster.

"You look well," Matthew said, now that we had some privacy from my friends.

"That's not what everyone else has been saying," I said, playing with the lock of hair framing the right side of my face. The scar on my cheek tingled. "I haven't been sleeping, my hand is still bandaged and hurts whenever I try to grab anything, and I've got old-lady bags under my eyes… I don't think I looked this bad after the accident."

"Why haven't you been sleeping?"

"Why do you think?" I snapped, then cowered at the sound of my own voice, quickly remembering who I was really talking to.

"I understand your world has been turned upside-down, but I'm here to help with that. You'll first learn how to defend yourself, then how to attack. We're strong, but not invincible. There is a lot of damage you can do with the right tools and knowhow."

"I've seen you out in the sunlight," I said, nervously glancing around, then leaning in and lowering my voice. "How is that possible for a… vampire?"

"Advancements in technology," Matthew said,

mirroring me by leaning into the metal table. "A compound commonly called sun serum, developed through extensive clinical trials with radiation sickness blocking agents, allows us to better battle the UV rays from the sun. It's still uncomfortable and we're still severely weakened in sunlight, but at least the serum allows us to function during a typical day. It is by no means a cure, mind you, but offers temporary relief."

"Is this something all vampires have access to?"

"Not all, but it's fairly accessible now. It can be purchased from large pharmaceutical companies, as well as street distributors. It's a major factor in the Vampire Nation movement."

"The Vampire Nation movement?"

"This is why you should have stuck around during training," Matthew said, but then seemed to regret saying it almost immediately. "There is a lot you need to learn—a lot happening as we speak, that most of the world is completely unattuned to. Have you ever noticed a small VN tattoo with a circle around it? It's usually red. Sometimes simply an encircled plus sign."

I thought about it but couldn't recall a specific instance of seeing one of those images on someone's body.

"And oftentimes, it's in a place that remains covered most of the time. It's not something usually advertised."

"Which may be why it doesn't ring a bell," I said. "What is it?"

"It's a brand for Vampire Nation—almost a cult-like group of individuals who want to be turned when the vampires decide to *come out*, so to speak. It shows their commitment to the cause and usually offers amnesty from fatal attacks."

"Do vampires in the group have that brand too?"

Matthew shook his head. "Vampires can't keep typical tattoos. Tattoos are like abrasions. Our skin heals them within seconds or minutes, causing them to disappear."

"But you have—"

"It's not a typical tattoo," he interjected. "It's a special proprietary brand developed specifically for the Society. You'll have to look at someone else's to see it in action; mine doesn't move." Matthew lifted his sleeve and showed me his forearm. "The north on mine always points up my arm—because I am a vampire. For everyone else, north points in the direction of the closest vampire, no matter how far away."

"The tattoo actually functions like a vampire compass?" I asked, extending my hand to touch his skin—his intricate tattoo again. But I stopped my hand just short of reaching him, afraid to touch him now.

Seeing my hesitation, Matthew grabbed my wrist

and guided my hand to his warm skin. "It's okay," he said, letting my wrist go.

I kept my fingers running down the palpable lines marking his otherwise perfect flesh, not breaking contact until I reached the base of his hand. A shiver ran up my arm, more of an electric current passing from one body to another rather than a product of fear. I returned my hand to my lap to conceal the shaking.

"Let's set up another training session for you tomorrow evening," Matthew said, straightening up in his chair. "Can you handle that?"

"I have to work tomorrow," I said with a frown. "But I'll see what I can do."

"Mallory!" he called, his sudden outburst catching me off guard.

I turned around in my chair and noticed her a few stores down, sitting at an outside table with friends. She looked up at the sound of her name, noticeably irritated by us trying to grab her attention. After leaning in to say something to her friends, she stood up and walked over to our table.

"Yes? Can I help you with something?" she asked, her attention solely on Matthew.

"I'd appreciate your help with getting Fiona's shift covered for tomorrow night."

"I can do it myself," I said.

"It's not really my job," Mallory said flatly.

"I'm making it your job, Mallory, since your

father owns the shop. I know you have a lot of pull when you want to," Matthew said. "You are a team player—right, candidate?"

"Of course," she said, without putting up more of an argument. "I'll take care of it."

"Thank you," Matthew said, giving her a satisfied smile.

"Sure," Mallory said and headed straight inside.

I gazed at him, awestruck. "You didn't have to do that."

Matthew shrugged and finished his coffee. "She needs to be humbled a little. And the two of you will need to find a way to work together—at least in some capacity."

"Doubtful," I said. "But I'll cooperate if she does."

"That's a start."

I checked my phone and saw that my break was already over; Eli would be out here any moment to give me the usual rhetorical question about my break. *How many minutes are in a ten-minute break?*

"I need to get back in," I said, standing and lifting the strap of my apron over my head.

"Do you want me to pick you up in the parking lot at eight tomorrow night?"

"That works for me," I said, then noticed Mallory standing in the doorway.

"It's all taken care of," she said, resentfully. "You're free to work on your fencing skills—God knows you need it. Is there anything else I can do for you?"

"Yes," Matthew said, handing her his empty coffee mug. "You can take this inside."

"One of our friendly baristas would love to do that for you," Mallory said, taking the mug and handing it to me, smirking as she spoke. "I'm not on the clock." And with that, she turned on her heel and marched back to her friends.

"Like I said—doubtful." I collected the two empty mugs, said goodnight to Matthew, and went back inside to finish my shift. Once inside the door, I glanced back just as Matthew stepped off the curb and into the parking lot. Our short interaction had somehow put me almost completely at ease. I had a good feeling I'd be able to sleep tonight, which sounded like absolute bliss.

FIONA

*T*he next afternoon, Matthew sent me a text to meet an hour earlier, so I did as he asked. When I saw the familiar black Land Rover park in the back of the lot, I hurried over. The passenger window descended, and I was greeted by a smiling Mallory. When I looked closer, I saw her coach, Aaron, behind the wheel.

"Get in," Aaron commanded.

"What's going on?" I asked, still a few feet away from the vehicle, afraid to come any closer.

"Matthew got held up with other matters and asked me to pick you up. We're all going to the same place. Let's go."

"Come on, Fiona," Mallory said, exasperated. "Stop being a baby."

"What about the other candidates?" I asked.

"They're not on the way; you were. Get in, candidate." Aaron gestured to the back door of the SUV.

When I still didn't come any closer, Mallory huffed out a loud sigh, got out, and opened the back door for me. "How much more of a formal invitation do you need?"

"I just want to give Matthew a call," I said, fighting to hold my ground.

"Call him in the car, so we don't continue to waste time."

And with that, I finally gave in and slid into the back seat. In a flash, Mallory was back in the front seat and we were maneuvering through the parking lot, leaving Hot Coffee behind.

As quickly as I could, I tried calling Matthew, but the call refused to connect. I couldn't even leave a message. I looked at the screen and found I had absolutely no bars.

"I'm getting no service," I said.

"Probably because your phone carrier sucks," Mallory said.

"Can I borrow yours?"

"Umm… no. You can talk to your vampire boyfriend soon enough. Calm down."

There never seemed to be a time I didn't want to strangle her, but now I knew she could kick my ass if I actually tried, which was even more frustrating.

In the seat next to me, I noticed a fancy department store bag. With nothing else to do, I opened it and found a new pair of dark blue jeans, a thin black top, and a box of shoes. The price tags were still attached, and I almost released an audible gasp when I read how much these clothes had cost. I'd never spent so much money on myself for anything in my whole life.

"What's this?" I asked.

"Oh, yeah," Aaron said. "Clothes for tonight. The training tonight involves a little field trip. You won't want to stand out too much for where we're going. The clothes are classy, yet inconspicuous. Go ahead and get changed."

"Where?" I asked, offended by his implication.

"In the back seat; where else? I'm not stopping. It's dark, so don't worry, no one's gonna see any of your lady bits."

I momentarily saw his eyes in the rearview mirror, then his attention returned to the road ahead.

"Where are we going?" I asked as I quickly removed my jeans and tugged and shimmied on the new pair of skinny jeans, having to suck in my stomach to button them up. I could barely breathe.

"I don't want to ruin the surprise," Aaron said, a hint of amusement in his voice, which only made me more nervous.

I tore the tag off the jeans hugging my lower body, then unfolded the top, which turned out to be a black short-sleeved turtleneck with an upside-down triangle cutout on the front and three more going down the back. The material was incredibly soft and felt wonderful on my skin. I watched Aaron and Mallory for another long moment before removing my tee shirt and sliding on the luxurious turtleneck. Lastly, I removed the lid of the shoebox and found a pair of black leather ankle-high boots with icepick thin heels. They looked dangerous—in more ways than one.

"You expect me to wear these?" I asked, holding one up.

"I expect you to dress the part," Aaron said as he turned onto the highway.

We took the 5 freeway north. It was past rush hour, but the freeway was still busy.

After a half hour of driving, I couldn't help but ask again. "Are you going to tell me where we're going now?"

"Okay; it's an exclusive club in the industrial district of South LA called Fangloria. It's not overly advertised. You probably haven't heard of it." He glanced into the rearview mirror.

"And why are we going there, exactly?"

"What does the name imply?"

"Vampires," I said.

"Correct. The candidate gets a gold star," he said with a hearty laugh. "There's a whole subculture of people fascinated by and obsessed with vampires, witches, the occult, bondage, and a whole slew of other darker fetishes. The supernatural stuff is all fantasy to the masses—but you've had your awakening. You know what lurks in the dark. Tonight, you'll get to see a little bit more of what the Society is up against—what society as a whole is up against. Have you heard of Vampire Nation?"

I thought back to the conversation with Matthew just last night. "Yes," I said.

"Good; then I don't have to explain it to you. What about the vamp stamp?"

"The what?"

"The tattoo of Vampire Nation—a red "VN" with a circle around it."

"Oh, yeah. Matthew told me about that too. And that it can also be a plus sign."

"Well look who's acing her midterm," Aaron said sarcastically. "Contrary to popular belief, the Vampire Nation movement was not started by a bunch of delusional goth kids. It was created by vampires—a select few interested in starting a new world order. Their leaders are helping vampires better infiltrate mainstream society at its highest levels—much like the True North Society has done. For now, they've intentionally kept their numbers low and most of them follow the guidance of the Vampire Order, which is the primary governing body of their kind. They are inconspicuously adding value everywhere you can think of—from scientific advancement, technological advancement, and corporate growth to various levels of government and special interests. What do you know of Damien Galt?"

"I've seen him on the news," I said. "He's some futurist billionaire, right?"

"He's also hailed as being the founder of the Vampire Nation movement. Of course, he'll never admit to that publicly."

"He's a vampire?"

"Like I said, those nasty bloodsuckers are all around us," Aaron said, and there was absolutely no sarcasm in his voice this time. That was how he truly felt. "When the movement finally decides to emerge from the underground—into the mainstream—it's believed he will be the one leading the charge."

"How do you know that's what he's planning?"

"We've got a pretty good track record of predicting the future too."

I could now see the towers of Los Angeles looming in the distance. Aaron turned onto the 101, and a few miles later, exited by the LA River. Concrete buildings, graffiti, and chained-linked fences topped with barbed wire were everywhere I looked. Vagrants sprawled out on the sidewalks, many bedding down in multi-colored tents, and many cars looked like they were junked years earlier. Streets lay in equal or greater disrepair than nearby buildings. Unsavory characters gathered around old vehicles and leaned against storefronts. I really hoped Aaron knew where he was going because I didn't want to be driving around here any longer than we had to.

After a few dilapidated blocks, we turned into a driveway blocked by a chain-linked gate characteristic of the area; two women loitered on either side of the driveway in dark, provocative outfits. They looked like high-class escorts, definitely not representative of the industrial neighborhood.

Aaron pulled up to the gate and rolled down his window. One of the women sauntered up to the driver's side. "May I help you? You look lost," the woman said in a rather deep voice.

"Fangloria," Aaron said without turning to look at her.

The woman bent down to rest her forearms atop the door, giving us all an eyeful of cleavage. Her gaze vacillated between the three of us—a predatory, hungry gaze. "Are you sure?"

I knew what I was looking at and the realization of being in such close proximity to another vampire turned my blood to ice.

Aaron turned to face her for the first time and provided a confident, "Yes."

"Then you should know what to do," she said and held out a delicate hand with long carmine nails. "Key and IDs, please."

I dug my license out of my purse and passed it up to Aaron, and Mallory did the same. The woman stepped back and straightened to full height with our IDs and some other card Aaron had added to the stack, then began saying something I couldn't hear. I glanced at the woman on the passenger side of the SUV who didn't look interested in us whatsoever. The woman with our IDs was not talking to her.

A few moments later, the first woman leaned back through the window and handed us the cards. Then she said, "You three have yourselves an eventful evening."

When she stepped away from the vehicle, the gate blocking the driveway rolled to one side, allowing us passage. It was a narrow drive between two concrete buildings. Another seemingly abandoned building directly ahead forced us to make a sharp left turn into an equally narrow space, but within a few hundred yards, that space opened to a large, half-empty parking lot.

"What was the key?" I asked.

But instead of answering my question, Aaron simply said, "Here we are."

"Where is it?" Mallory asked.

"Like I said, it's not advertised."

On the far side of the parking lot, a man and woman were standing by an open nondescript door. A small group of women was approaching it, all dressed for an expensive night on the town. Tight clothing and hooker heels. I peered down at the clothing I was now wearing and realized I was in no place to judge.

Many of the cars parked around us were as expensive-looking as Aaron's Land Rover, some of them more so. A limousine was even parked lengthwise against the building over to the right.

"Now your total immersion training begins," Aaron said after he'd turned off the engine.

There are more of them in there. The sentence kept repeating in my head, on the verge of hyperventilating.

I checked my phone again, but still there was no service. "Where's Matthew?" I asked. "Or the other candidates?"

"If they're not already in there, then they'll be arriving soon. Not to worry. We're not going to start any trouble and the vampires aren't going to, either. If anything, it's other humans we may have to worry about, but the vampire employees of the club will defuse any situation before it gets out of hand. They want to avoid bad press. Now, they won't allow phones inside, so I'd leave them here if I were you. I don't trust my phone in their possession."

"Fine," Mallory said and stashed her phone in the glove compartment.

I stowed mine in my purse, which I then slid under the front seat. I couldn't help but feel naked without it. I was so anxious to see Matthew, desperate to get out from under Aaron's alleged protection.

We exited the SUV and made our way to the open door. Techno music from inside the club could be heard clearly from the parking lot. I stepped carefully, trying to avoid any holes or cracks in the concrete that might catch a toothpick heel. The last thing I needed was to break an ankle.

Once we reached the two attendants at the door, we were asked to show our IDs again. The man who examined mine must've been nearly seven feet tall because he towered over Mallory and me even in our high heels. He had long limbs, a rugged, angular face, and long brown hair. He flexed my driver's license back and forth a few times before returning it.

"Any weapons?" he asked in a gruff voice.

"No," I replied.

"Cellphone?"

"No."

"Arms out. Legs apart."

I did as I was told, and he proceeded to pat me down. I flinched when his strong, exploratory hands grazed some of my more intimate areas.

"Turn around."

Again, I complied, and he repeated the process from the back.

"You're clean," he said, drew a large X on the back of my right hand—the one without the bandage—in permanent marker, then stepped aside, allowing me to pass.

Aaron and Mallory were already waiting for me at the mouth of a dark hallway. Mallory had a similar marking on her right hand, her left still bandaged like mine. Black lights lined the ceiling. The tunnel we were entering amplified the thumping bass and synthetic soundscapes from inside.

We stepped up to a box office, where Aaron paid the cover charge for himself; apparently Mallory and I were getting in free. Next, we passed a coat check closet where a blonde woman in a top hat, tuxedo jacket with long tails, white shirt with bowtie, and black tights sat patiently on a stool, awaiting her next customer. It wasn't that cold outside, but there were more coats lining the wall than I would've guessed.

Aaron noticed my inquisitive look and said, "To conceal what many of these women are *not* wearing." And after my expression didn't change, he added, "If you came wearing only lingerie, you'd bring a coat too."

My eyes widened in shock and embarrassment.

"What? Not an exhibitionist?" Mallory laughed. "Maybe you're a voyeur."

"I guess we'll find out," Aaron said, joining in on the laughter.

FIONA

*A*aron guided us the rest of the way inside, which opened into a dark, sprawling underground-looking lounge with multiple bars and half-moon sofas. From the flashing lights coming from another tunnel, it seemed the dance floor was on the opposite side. The floor was nearly concealed with a low-hanging fog. Up higher was merely hazy, making the LED lights on the open industrial ceiling look like lasers shooting down into the fog.

Many of the people filling the couches—women and men—were in various stages of undress. And as Aaron had said, several women I could see were dressed in nothing but lingerie, enticing their suitors with more than just a little extra skin.

As we wandered deeper into the lounge, I spotted my first Vampire Nation tattoo, exactly as Mathew had described it—a red VN with a circle around the acronym—prominently displayed on one woman's collarbone. That told me the woman was human… and most likely the man she was conversing with was a… vampire. I shuddered as he glanced up at us while we walked by.

It soon became a game of how many more tattoos I could spot, and they began to pop up everywhere like a new blouse you just bought that seemed so unique at the store.

"I don't see anyone familiar," I said, when Aaron stopped to scan the room.

"You're right. I'm going to make a few inquiries. Hold tight," he said and walked away from Mallory and me.

I nervously glanced around the room, at the not-so-subtle debauchery taking place in every darkened corner of the lounge. "What are we supposed to do now?" I asked Mallory, who was focused in another direction.

"I'm gonna get a drink while we wait," Mallory said and headed for the closest bar.

I never thought I'd be in a situation where I'd rather follow her than be left on my own, but this turned out to be it. As much as I loathed Mallory Fiennes, I was petrified to be left alone in this precarious club of vampires and fanatics—whom Aaron at one point had called *vanatics*. I hurried after

Mallory, careful to remain steady on my heels, something she seemed to have no issue with. She was obviously a lot more practiced than me in a great many things.

She approached two empty stools as they were vacated by a sinister-looking couple. I refused to look the leaving couple in the eyes as I took the stool beside Mallory.

"Let me see your hands," the bartender demanded when Mallory got his attention.

"Seltzer water with lime," she said.

He nodded and glanced at me.

"I—I'll take the same," I said.

"So typical," Mallory commented under her breath, not bothering to look at me.

I wasn't about to fight with her here, but also wasn't about to engage her in small talk. So, once we received our drinks, we sat at the bar in relative silence.

On the wall behind the bar, I noticed a framed picture of the man Aaron had mentioned on the drive here—Damien Galt—shaking hands with the President. The thought of what he really was, chilled me to my core. How could someone so popular and influential be one of *them*? I was still trying to get used to the fact that some of these supernatural beings existed. It was one thing to have them lurking in the dark, but so much more terrifying to know they were seamlessly interwoven into our society. The fact that this club existed served as one more reminder that they were all around us.

"There's no need to be nervous; we don't bite."

I gave the man seated beside me a sidelong glance and he greeted me with a wide, disarming smile. He had icy blue eyes and short black hair and was wearing a violet dress shirt with the top two buttons undone. He didn't flash his fangs, but the hair standing up on the back of my neck told me exactly what he was—not to mention the glass of crimson liquid set before him. He was as striking as the others in the club, with his age just as deceptive. My throat was instantly dry, but I couldn't move to take a sip from my water.

"Without permission, that is," the man said, leaning into me, his smile widening on his porcelain-skinned face.

"I'm...umm...not one of those girls..." I stammered.

"Just because you're not marked doesn't mean you're not curious," he said.

My hands shook against my cold glass. "I... uhh..."

"I don't mean to make you feel uncomfortable, sweetling. This is a magical place where everyone can be themselves—a place where you can escape, indulge, explore..." He picked up his glass and brought it closer to me. "Cheers. May you find what you're looking for."

"Thank you," I said, weakly. "Same to you."

"I'm certain we both shall." He took a sip. "I noticed you looking at the picture on the wall. I'm assuming you're familiar with the man with the President. Am I right?"

"I know of him. Damien Galt," I said. "I hear he's not who he appears to be."

"Indeed. But which of us is…?"

"Let's go, ladies."

I was so relieved to hear the voice of Aaron. I instantly spun in my stool to face him.

"You can take your drinks with you," he said.

"Is Matthew here?" I asked, stepping down from the stool.

"On his way," Aaron said.

"Enjoy your evening," said the man who'd been sitting next to me.

I glanced back and gave him a weak smile as he once again raised his nearly-drained glass to me.

Aaron led us through the crowd, into another room serving as a dancefloor. Several scantily-clad women danced on raised podiums. Glitter and gems on their skin made them sparkle, multi-colored light refracting off their bodies like seductive disco balls.

"Already making friends, I see," Aaron yelled as we made our way around the perimeter of the room.

"He was talking to *me*," I clarified.

"Sure," he laughed as we entered another tunnel, then an adjoining lounge.

On the far side of the lounge was a closed door with the backlit words, "The Cellar" above it. Aaron headed straight for it and held the door open, ushering us to continue down the dimly lit staircase. Mock torches with flickering LEDs hung on the stone walls like we were entering a medieval dungeon.

There was softer music down here—classical, stringed music—with almost no bleed through from the pulsating electronic music upstairs. Each descending click of our heels seemed to echo in the room below, announcing to everyone that we were coming. My heart was pounding in rhythm with my footfalls, terrified of what new sights awaited us.

I knew I couldn't prepare myself for what the cellar housed, but when we stepped out of the staircase, my heartbeat increased threefold. Stretched out before us was a massive open room with rows of crescent moon couches, which half encircled bottom-lit podiums no higher than the couch cushions. And attached to the podiums were large wooden X's. The ones that were occupied had a girl or guy chained to the Xs, bodies spread wide to mimic the letters themselves. And those chained individuals had one or more vampires paying them special attention, while others watched the attacks or performances from the couches.

There must have been twenty or thirty couch setups, most of them occupied. There were no screams, but plenty of moaning and groaning of pleasure or anguish contributed to the room's sickening ambiance.

I turned abruptly and ran straight into Aaron, who caught me with both hands, clutching my upper arms, trying to minimize the spillage from my water glass.

"Whoa, slow down," he said.

"What is this? What are we doing here?" I asked, barely able to get the words out. The glass shook in my hand.

"You both need to see what we're up against. The temptation. The vile savagery." He spun me around and pushed me further into the room.

Mallory remained at my side as we walked down an aisle, podiums lining either side. My eyes darted back and forth—at the fragile-looking prisoners at the mercy of their heinous masters. Many of the bound humans were in their underwear, the rest of their clothes in haphazard piles on the floor, so access to their skin was plentiful. There was ripped lingerie, blood, tears, ecstasy, and the lustful eyes of audience members on the couches. To my horror, I identified more tattoos.

Halfway down the aisle, Aaron pulled at my arm,

signaling Mallory and me to stop. We stood before a couch with four men seated on it and an empty podium. I glanced nervously at the men on the couch, desperately hoping to recognize someone— but all four shadowed figures were strangers.

"Gentlemen, may I introduce to you Fiona Winter and my little sister, Mallory," Aaron said.

I was so shocked by the words that just escaped his lips that I momentarily forgot about the men on the couch. I glanced back at him, my mouth agape, while he smiled down at me.

"It's nice to meet you, Fiona," someone said, forcing me to return my attention to the new men in our company. A large man with arms as thick as my thighs was now standing before me, hand extended for me to shake.

Apprehensively, I met his hand, which engulfed mine completely. And the next thing I knew, he was pulling me toward him, his grip like an iron mana- cle. A second man leapt up from the couch and grabbed my other wrist, knocking my water glass to the floor. Between both men, they easily heaved me up onto the lit podium, forcing each wrist into a leather cuff on each arm of the X.

I screamed as I struggled for freedom, but I was securely locked in—the wooden X barely moving an inch. And before my screams could turn to pleas, a ball gag was thrust into my mouth and strapped to the back of my head.

"We can't have you disturbing the other patrons," the first man said into my ear.

Tears streamed down my face, as I was unsure of what was happening to me. Where was Matthew? Was this a test of the True North Society? I didn't want this—this was not how I wanted to get in! My whole body turned ice cold when the first man cupped my cheek with one bear-sized hand. Then I felt hands on my right ankle as it was strapped to the bottom right leg of the X. Once my left ankle was also secured, the second man returned to the couch, leaving me with the big guy who'd first shaken my hand.

Unable to cry for help, I watched as Mallory stepped up onto the podium and stopped before me, her expression grim and eyes smoldering. Then she reached forward, her perfectly manicured hand reaching into the top of the turtleneck and clawing at my skin beneath. Having found what she was looking for, Mallory pulled out the compass pendant I had received from Matthew. She gripped it tightly in her fist and tugged, snapping the chain and freeing it from my neck.

"You don't deserve to wear this," she snarled. "Don't delude yourself into thinking you're one of us."

Turning on her stiletto heel, Mallory stepped down from the platform and joined Aaron in walking toward the stairs. They were... leaving me here. I screamed into the ball gag, which was enough to get Mallory's attention one last time. She twisted just enough to glance back, gave me a small wave, then followed her coach—her brother—up the staircase, leaving me with monsters far worse than any of my nightmares could conjure.

FIONA

*a*s horrible a person as she was, how could she leave me here? What kind of a human being would do that to another? If only I'd never accepted the call of the True North Society. I'd still have been living my normal life—going to school, working my shifts at Hot Coffee, and complaining about the boss's daughter with my best friends. I would not have been subjected to this...

I tugged at the leather cuffs on my wrists, but it was no use. I couldn't escape and couldn't protect myself from the incoming assaults. My legs shook and were losing strength, but the bindings held me in place, not even allowing me to collapse to the floor. The only escape I could hope for, was passing out quickly.

The large man standing before me grabbed at my turtleneck with both hands and effortlessly ripped it right down the center. Smiling, he moved the material away from my neck and ran his rough fingers over my bare skin, sending shivers surging through my body. I closed my eyes, still brimming with tears, waiting for him to take his first bite. Cold air gently washed over the skin exposed by my open shirt. I pictured the man's face inches from me, breathing steadily on my skin, breathing in my scent like a feral animal.

But still nothing was happening. When I finally gathered the courage to open my eyes and blink away some of the tears, I discovered I was alone on the podium. My would-be attackers were now engaged in conversation with the man I'd met at the bar.

"What part of *willing participants* do you not understand?" the man from the bar asked, glaring at each of the four men from the couch. "This is not the kind of behavior I condone in my establishment. I don't need another raid due to dirtbags like you."

"It was just a little joke, nothing more," the guy with the bear hands said.

"Does it look like she's laughing? Did I miss the joke? Maybe I'm too dumb to get it. Is that it?" The man from upstairs was now wholly focused on the big male with the bear hands. Then with both hands, the man from the bar grabbed the big man's head, and with a sickening crunch, twisted it around 180 degrees.

I shrieked in horror as the big man crumpled to the ground, his friends all taking a few steps back, refusing to put up a fight for their lost friend. I quickly looked away, afraid I was about to throw up into the ball gag—and potentially drown in it. Stars swirled around me even with my eyes closed. I began to heave but fought to keep the contents down.

"Remove that ball gag before she throws up," the man from the bar said.

Moments later, the rubber ball was pulled out of my mouth. I continued to heave, enough so that I tasted the wretchedness rise to the back of my throat. But still I swallowed it down, cringing at the lingering bitterness.

Next, my arms were freed, then my legs. I fell forward, but was caught by two of the men on the way down, who carried me over to the couch.

"I suggest you heed the rules of my establishment, or next time none of you will be leaving here alive," the man from the bar warned in a menacing tone. "Now leave us. And leave *him*."

I tried not to think of the dead body at my feet. Slowly, the bursting stars in my vision began to recede. Now I could see the other groups on nearby couches, all eyes on the situation unfolding at our unlucky station.

When the other three men had fled, the man from the bar stepped over the body on the floor and sat a person's distance away from me on the couch. "Are you okay?" he asked, sounding genuinely concerned. "I apologize for the situation you were forced into. It is not something I condone."

"This is *your* club?" I asked, my voice scratchy and hoarse.

"It is," he said. "Allow me to introduce myself. My name is Frederick Alabaster." He offered me his hand.

Trying not to think too much about what that hand had just done, I quickly shook it and strained to pull mine back, but he held it longer than expected. Then he brought it to his lips and gently kissed my knuckles.

"I could see upstairs that you were new to this. Just know we're not all so terrible," Frederick said, and only then released my hand. "May I have the pleasure of your name?"

"F—Fiona," I said, my body still shaking. I clasped my hands together and shoved them into my lap.

"Well, Fiona, it seems the friends you arrived with are not great friends at all."

I shook my head in agreement.

"You will most likely be needing a ride home. Do you have a cellphone checked in upstairs?"

I shook my head again.

"In that case, is there a friend we can call, or simply a taxi to pick you up?"

I wanted to call Matthew, but didn't have his

number memorized and my phone was still in Aaron's Land Rover—along with my clothes. I didn't know if they were really gone or were just waiting upstairs, but there was no way I was getting in a car with them again. I thought of calling Alexis or Candace, but didn't want them to pick me up here. I shouldn't even have thought of subjecting them to this hellish underbelly of society.

"A taxi will work," I said, softly. "If it's not too much trouble."

"It's the least I can do," Frederick said. "I'd offer to drive you home myself, but I'd bet that would make you even more uncomfortable."

I silently thanked him for not insisting on that, then said, "Thank you for helping me."

"I hate to see someone not enjoying themselves in my club. When you're ready and willing to experience more, then you should really consider coming back."

I adamantly doubted that, and my stomach lurched just from the thought of ever setting foot in here again, but I couldn't express that, so I simply nodded and produced the best smile I could manage given the circumstances.

Frederick made a call on his cell phone—obviously given special treatment with being the owner —to have the body of the man with the bear hands disposed of and to call a taxi. Then he walked me back upstairs to the pounding music and rooms of scantily clad patrons. He walked purposefully through the crowds, who continually parted for him like the Red Sea. I fought to remain in his wake as we made our way to the main entrance.

As I left the confines of the vampire club and entered the industrial night air, I was finally able to fully breathe, despite the staleness outside. I was still alive—unharmed actually—and had everything to be grateful for, thanks to the man walking before me.

However, Frederick stopped abruptly as we reached the parking lot, his gaze intensely focused on someone swiftly approaching us. As his face came into the moonlight, I saw it was Matthew, and my heart leapt at the sight of him.

MATTHEW

I saw Frederick before noticing Fiona and was immediately afraid this was it—the end of her. I had no idea why he'd spare her when he hadn't spared any of the previous women in my life, but I prayed she'd become that exception.

They were heading into the parking lot of Fangloria, but Frederick halted when he saw me coming. A sly grin spread over his face while he waited for me to close the gap between us.

"Matthew!" Fiona exclaimed when she finally recognized me.

She didn't look physically injured but did look like she'd been through hell. Her black turtleneck was ripped down the center. Her eyes were bloodshot, dirty streaks lining her cheeks.

"Is this another friend of yours?" Frederick asked, innocently.

"Yes," Fiona said. "I'll go with him."

"If you're sure." Frederick kept his eyes trained on me.

"Fiona, are you all right?" I asked, once I was standing before the two of them.

"Please just take me home," she pleaded.

"I'll cancel the taxi," Frederick said.

Fiona turned to him. "I really do appreciate your help."

Frederick reached out and shook her hand, and it took all my self-control not to rip her away from him. "It was a pleasure to be of service, sweetling," Frederick said, then kissed her knuckles. His gaze wandered to me as he released her, his smile unfaltering.

I pointed my clicker at the sea of cars, punching the button to make the lights flash on my Land Rover. "Fiona, go wait in the car. And lock the door," I commanded.

She didn't need to be told twice and hurried past me in the direction of the Land Rover.

"I didn't expect to have you grace us with your presence," Frederick said.

"What did you do to her?" I snarled.

"Me? I saved your nubile princess from a night of humiliation and bloodletting," Frederick said. "Is she your latest obsession?"

"Don't patronize me. I know it was you," I said, sticking my index finger directly in his face. "And when I can prove it, I'll be back to pay you a visit. You will not lay a finger on her again."

"You're always so dramatic, Matthew," Frederick said. "You should know by now your threats amount to nothing. As always, we can talk things out like the civilized individuals we are."

"This isn't over!" I warned.

"Why don't you come in for a drink? On the house. She'll be fine in the car for a little while."

"Stay away from her," I said.

"It's not my fault she got thrust into my lap," Frederick said with a smirk. "You may have to work harder to keep her away from *me*."

"I'm warning you!" I roared, getting right up in his face, baring my fangs.

"It's always a pleasure to see you, Matthew. Don't stay away so long next time," Frederick said, flashing a predatory grin, then casually headed back into his nightclub.

Now, I was convinced Frederick was behind Fiona's accident, though I still didn't know if it had been intended to kill her or serve as a warning. I suspected it was his way of saying she was on his radar and that he'd toy with her—and thus toy with me—as he pleased, in whichever manner he saw fit. And now, he was appealing to Fiona's emotional distress as her savior, attempting to make me look crazy and paranoid. But I knew I was neither of those things, having witnessed over the decades the savagery and depravity he was truly capable of.

I marched back to the Land Rover and climbed into the driver's seat. "Are you hurt?" I asked as I started the ignition.

Fiona shook her head as she stared out into the night, out at the brightly lit high rises of Los Angeles towering over the forgotten industrial buildings in this derelict neighborhood. "Frederick saved me before anything bad happened," she said after a prolonged silence. "Where were you?"

Before I even had the chance to answer, Fiona broke down in tears—a deluge of emotion from the unexpected evening suddenly pouring out of her. I offered her a packet of tissues from the glove compartment and allowed her to cleanse her system while I accelerated onto the freeway. I didn't know if my touch would help or hurt, so I kept my hands on the wheel to give her the space she seemed to need. I knew her world would never be the same, and she was still realizing it.

It took a while, but she finally calmed—the tears drying up, her breathing steadying as we left the horrors of the city behind. It wasn't until then that I answered her question.

"My phone was hacked," I said. "The text changing the meeting time didn't come from me. By the time I found out what had happened and who was responsible, the Land Rover Aaron had taken was already at the club, so I sped here as quickly as I could."

"Couldn't you have just run here in a flash—gotten here in like a minute or two?"

"You've been watching too many movies," I said with a laugh. "I'm fast for short distances, but not *that* fast."

"Aaron is Mallory's brother..." She wiped her eyes with another wadded tissue. "Why didn't you tell me?"

"I didn't realize you didn't know. It wasn't like it was a secret. Hasn't he been around the coffee shop, since his father owns it?"

"I've never seen him there," Fiona said. "They have my purse and phone... and my clothes. Oh, and my necklace."

"He took your True North necklace?" I didn't know what I was going to do when I saw Aaron next —or maybe even his father, Douglas. That family had crossed so many lines tonight. I loathed the thought of having to continue to put up with them— but knew, even as livid as I was, the events of tonight weren't going to ultimately change anything with them. As much as I wanted to kill the lot of them, I knew I couldn't. My next challenge was to keep Fiona from quitting after this little stunt.

"Mallory took it," Fiona answered.

"I'm so sorry about tonight," I said. "I knew the two of you were at odds, but I didn't realize it was this bad. As hard as it's going to be, you're going to have to somehow find a way to work together."

"You're asking for the impossible," Fiona said.

"Like the existence of angels and vampires? *That* kind of impossible?"

"More so," she said, defiantly, crossing her arms and adjusting her bangs to adequately frame her face—what she always did when she wanted to hide.

However, as adamant as she was at being unable to work with Mallory, she didn't sound like she was giving up, which gave me hope. Maybe she wouldn't need convincing after all.

A short while later, Fiona was asleep in the passenger seat, her head bobbing to one side when we hit bumps in the road. I reached for the controls to recline her chair, but fell a few inches short. Even though she didn't look overly comfortable, she looked peaceful for the first time.

I DIDN'T WAKE her until we were parked in her apartment complex. Though I tried my best not to startle her, she jerked violently in her seat, arms flying up in front of her face like she was anticipating an attack.

"Hey. It's only me," I said, keeping my distance.

It still took her a moment to remember where she was and that she was safe in my company. While she fought to return to calmness, I exited the vehicle, walked around to her door, and opened it.

"I'll get your stuff back," I promised.

"Okay."

I offered my hand to help her step down from the passenger seat. She'd discarded the heels sometime after we'd gotten on the highway, having thrown them in the back seat. She was now barefoot. Fiona took my hand and dropped down onto the concrete.

As soon as our hands parted, she snaked her arms around my waist and rested her head on my chest. I was initially taken aback, but then wrapped my arms around her small body. Her hair smelled like an exotic mixture of fruit from whatever shampoo she used. Every bit of her was intoxicating and I could feel my fangs yearning to be set free. I pushed at them with my tongue to keep them at bay.

Upon letting go, she gazed up into my eyes and said, "Thank you." Our connection lingered for multiple heavy heartbeats, then she broke away and hurried across the parking lot to her apartment, leaving me breathless, aching, and incredibly thirsty.

30

FIONA

I was home earlier than I would have been if I'd worked a normal closing shift. The closed kitchen blinds glowed, signaling that Mom was home. I didn't think my luck was good enough to get from the front door to my room unseen, so I didn't even try.

I unlocked the door and entered the apartment as usual. Mom looked up from one of the couches, reading glasses low on her nose and an e-reader in her lap. One look at me caused her to remove her glasses and stare at me.

"What are you wearing? And what happened to your shoes?" she asked, trying to mask her concern with the hopes that I had an innocent, logical explanation.

Of course, I didn't—and was too emotionally

drained to come up with one. "I don't want to talk about it."

"You told me you were working tonight."

"I did, but… didn't. I mean, I got my shift covered so I could go out with the girls. Alexis lent me the clothes. I forgot my shoes in her car." I closed the front door and strolled into the kitchen. "Can we not do twenty questions right now? I'm really spent."

While I rummaged through the pantry cabinet, Mom appeared at the edge of the kitchen. "What happened to your shirt? If you tell me you're okay, I'll believe you. But I want you to know I'm here to talk if you need to."

I glanced down at the ripped front of the turtle-neck, vividly remembering what the damage signi-fied. "I'm fine, Mom," I said, then snatched the carton of Oreos from the cabinet.

"You know you shouldn't be eating those at this hour," she admonished.

"I know; I'm gonna blow up like a damn balloon," I snapped, rolling my eyes as I pushed past her.

"I'm not calling you fat, kid," she shot back. "I just want you to have healthy eating habits. I know I didn't always train you right when you were younger."

"A few cookies aren't going to kill me."

"You're right, *a few* won't."

"I can't deal with this right now." I stormed off to my room and made a point of slamming the door. I dropped onto the bed and watched the door to see if Mom was going to come in after me, unwilling to let me off the hook so easily. After a few minutes of waiting, I decided she'd let me have my space and I finally got comfortable by peeling off the wretched clothes I'd been given and slipping into my pajamas.

Looking down at my hand, I wanted to scrub off the X—the other horrid reminder of where I'd been this evening, but I didn't want to leave the illusory safety of my room.

So instead, I opened the carton of Oreos and split the first cookie. I laid the naked half beside me on the comforter and popped the filling half into my mouth. The familiar sweetness flirted with my taste buds and helped me feel truly at home. As quickly as the first cookie disappeared, another had taken its place, then another.

After a few more Oreos, I started to feel sick, also a familiar feeling. I curled up on the bed and pulled the open bag closer. Each time another vision of the vampires in The Cellar entered my mind, I took another bite. I could still feel their hands on my skin as they secured me to the X-shaped posts. I could still hear the moans of pleasure coming from the nearby couches and podiums, making me even more nauseous. My heart was racing from the vivid memories, as well as the sugar rush.

Then it wasn't just about the vampires and their horrific nature, but about the people I was supposed to be able to trust in this new society I'd become entangled in. Of course, I knew better than to trust Mallory—I'd known her true nature for years as we'd grown up together. Matthew had said this process was supposed to be giving us a new bond, one that rose above petty likes and dislikes, but I knew that would never be the case between Mallory and me; here, we shared no salvation. However, now I was afraid the rift between us could prevent me becoming a full-fledged True North member, ultimately causing me to lose any and all access to my father. I'd had no real luck searching for him on my own. I'd feared the Society might be my only chance —and that Mallory was doing everything in her power to keep me out.

"I wish I could still have some," Becca said, her voice so envious of the stack of half Oreos I'd constructed on my comforter. "They look so good."

"I know; it's probably mean of me to still be saving your half," I said. "But I can't help it. I can't bring myself to eat them. God, I think I'm gonna throw up."

"Why are you still eating?"

"I don't know," I said. "It seems every part of my life is out of control. I can't even control my Oreo consumption."

"Why are you so upset?"

"I told you about that bi—umm, awful girl, Mallory. Well, she's upped her awfulness to a whole new level. I don't think I can continue to deal with her."

"Then don't. Get away from her."

"I can't, Becks," I said. "If I quit the group I told you about, then I won't be able to find out about Dad."

"What's more important?"

"Stop getting all smart on me," I laughed. "I can't control my search for him any more than I can control anything else. He owes us an explanation. And no one else is gonna get that out of him." I went to pull apart another Oreo, then stopped and willed myself to place it back in the carton.

"See? You can do it when you want to."

"My desire to not want to clean up vomit finally surpassed my desire to make myself sick. I wouldn't really call that self-control. Remember when things were simple? When there were just people and ghosts?"

"Have you met other ghosts?" Becca asked.

"No; Becks. Just you," I said. "Now, there are vampires and angels going about their lives in the world like it's perfectly normal."

"Maybe it is," she said.

"It's insane," I argued. I removed my pillow from under my head and gave it a squeeze. "I wish you were here, so I could hug you." The threat of tears stung my eyes. "I really do."

"But I am here," Becca said.

"I know. I just need someone to hold me and tell me everything's going to be all right."

"Everything's gonna be all right," Becca whispered.

"I love you, Becks."

"Love you too, Fee."

I closed my eyes, imaging Becca right beside me. I squeezed her tight. Then that image turned into Matthew, and I continued to squeeze, my arms tight around his rock-solid body. Despite how those creatures terrified me, he somehow made me feel safe in this crazy new world—a world I barely recognized anymore.

31

MATTHEW

I returned to the headquarters on a mission. From tracking Aaron's SUV, I knew he'd returned it and had a good feeling he was still in the building. I stormed through the hallways to the office he shared with three other Society members, all of similarly new ranking.

I barged into the office without the slightest care about who else I'd find. Inside, Aaron was laughing with Zelda's coach, his friend, Charles Anderson. Their laughter quickly died down at the sight of me in the doorway.

"Too good to knock?" Aaron asked, his face growing cold as his smile faded.

"Where's her stuff?" I demanded.

"I should probably get going," Anderson said, rising from his chair.

"No need; this will only take a moment," Aaron

said, opening the bottom drawer of his desk and removing a crumpled plastic bag. He tossed the bag to me and kicked the drawer shut. "There you go. Her clothes are even neatly folded. You're welcome."

I snatched the bag out of the air with one hand, then opened it to examine the contents. The clothes and purse were obvious, but I had to dig through the bag to find the necklace, which had fallen into the toe of one shoe. The clasp on the chain was broken, which made me even more furious.

Satisfied everything was accounted for, I set the bag on the closest desk and approached Aaron. I grabbed his neck with one hand and lifted him straight into the air. I could crush his windpipe with little effort, so I slightly squeezed to remind him of that simple fact.

Aaron clawed at my hands, drawing blood, but the pain meant nothing to me.

"What do you have to say for yourself!" I roared, then dropped him back into his chair, which tipped over, spilling him to the carpeted floor.

Anderson quickly slipped by, but I let him go, not giving a damn who he told. I'd make sure Aaron answered for what he'd done, no matter what.

Aaron coughed and spluttered there on the floor, fighting to regain control of his breathing. Then he crawled to his desk and yanked open the bottom drawer, ripping it off its hinges. Inside, he grabbed a filled shoulder holster and fumbled to free the handgun. When he did, I kicked it right out of his hand. The Society-issued weapon ricocheted off the far wall.

"Your tools aren't going to save you now," I said, squatting to his level.

"You never did have a sense of humor," Aaron said, between coughing fits. "It was just a joke. She was never in any real danger; she was in good hands."

"You have no idea what you did," I growled. "You practically signed her death warrant."

"I know she's your new pet project, but she shouldn't be here. We don't owe her entry—ask anyone. We only had this final candidate class for my sister. If it wasn't for her, there'd be no candidate class."

"No! You and your father can pretend you're running things all you want, but the reality is, you're not. Fiona was always going to be a candidate, and she'll be initiated, just like your sister."

"But my sister makes it onto the station; Fiona doesn't. It's in the old logs. What does that tell you?"

"It tells me you're trying to tamper with something far greater than you and it's going to be your downfall." I grabbed him by the face, ready to snap his jaw like kindling. "If you ever pull a stunt like that again, I will—"

"Matthew, let him go!" someone yelled from behind me.

I shoved Aaron's head to the floor and stood up. When I turned to see who was challenging me, I was surprised to find Vladimir pointing a handgun at me. I was sure he had wood-encased hollow-point bullets—sleeper bullets—sure to drop me if he was lucky enough to hit anything vital. Behind him stood Douglas Fiennes and Ashley Degray. Aaron's father looked like he was about to have an aneurism.

"I didn't do anything he didn't deserve," I said.

"This is just another example of why you should be stripped of your tattoo and terminated!" Douglas shouted. "You can't be trusted!"

"Your kids abandoned my candidate at Fangloria!" I shot back. "You want to talk about *unacceptable?*"

"Matthew, I need to know you're in control," Vladimir said, his gun still trained on me.

"I'm good," I said, throwing up my hands in surrender.

"If you ever touch either of my children again, I will put a sleeper in your heart myself," Douglas warned.

"And if they screw with my candidate again, I'll come straight for you," I growled, flashing my fangs.

"You do that, and I'll put you down like the rabid dog you are."

"Shut up, Douglas," Ashley said. "We're all on the same side."

"No, Ashley. I'm tired of you playing the mediator. This animal needs to be controlled."

I snatched the plastic bag from the desk and marched toward the guarded doorway, ready to barrel through the three of them if need be. "If you'll excuse me, I need to return the personal items your kids stole from *my* candidate."

They all saw how serious I was and stepped aside, even though I knew a part of Douglas wanted to antagonize me further to coax me to attack him. However, he simply glared at me, and I snarled back like the animal he wanted me to be.

Halfway down an adjacent hallway, I heard my name being called by an old friend as she tried to catch up to me. Now in her seventies, she didn't get around as freely as she used to, but she was still in relatively good health.

"Matthew, wait up," Ashley called.

"I don't need to be chastised right now," I said, stopping, but refusing to turn and face her.

"Then stop playing right into his hands." She walked around to face me since I wouldn't turn. "I try to help you wherever I can, but you're making it more and more difficult to defend you. I know you mean well, but outbursts need to be controlled when it comes to our own members—members of the Assembly. Go take your aggression out elsewhere."

"I know all this," I said.

"Perhaps you should stop depriving yourself of

human blood; I think it's clouding your judgement," Ashley said. When I did nothing more than shrug, she continued. "I know you feel strongly about Fiona getting in. We promised Roland we'd extend her an invitation years ago when she came of age, but she's not worth getting yourself into more trouble for. She's just another girl. Remember, you're more important than she is."

"She's important too," I said, sounding defeated.

"If you say so," she said, nonchalantly. "What aren't you telling me? What is it about this girl, that makes it so personal?"

"I'd rather not discuss this. You'll just have to trust me one more time."

"We've come this far." Ashley folded her arms across her chest. "So, what are we going to do? You know Douglas will report this incident to the Assembly."

"And I'll be more than happy to defend myself in the conference room." When she eyed me suspiciously, I added, "*Through discussion.*"

"They're not going to agree to admit quarreling candidates—even with them being legacies."

"Then what do you suggest?"

"You're not going to like it, and Douglas will have an absolute fit. They need to be forced to rely on each other—deny them of any other options."

"You're right; I don't like the sound of this," I said, but heard her out with an open mind.

FIONA

Several days later, I was back in the training gymnasium, fencing with Mallory. I'd hoped with the recent history between us, that they'd at least have paired us up differently. But no such luck. We seemed to be stuck together.

Aaron and Matthew watched our sparring from opposite sides of the mat. Tensions appeared to be high with them too.

Again, Mallory was able to best me every time, oftentimes in the span of a few seconds. But occasionally, I was able to fend her off for a minute or more before her superior skill forced me into submission.

"You just don't know when to quit, do you?" Mallory said as she jabbed the button tip of the sabre into my chest. "*Dead.*"

"Your determination to get me to quit is the

biggest thing keeping me going," I retorted, getting back to my feet.

Before we started again, the trainer, Vladimir, stopped and adjusted my stance. "Don't hold your wrist so rigid. Flowing movements, like a dance." He stepped back and said, "Begin."

Vladimir watched as I got my ass handed to me again.

"Yes; just keep doing that," Mallory said. I could sense the smile behind her mask. "Can't I practice with someone who actually knows what she's doing?"

Vladimir requested my sabre and asked me to step aside, so I joined Matthew at the edge of the mat and removed my mask.

"I don't think you understand how embarrassing this is," I said as Mallory and Vladimir began to spar, looking like seasoned champions.

"Right now, you're simply proving your desire and commitment to being here," Matthew said. "The skill will come in time."

"I don't care about that, but she's actively trying to make me look like a fool. It's what she's always done."

"You don't look like a fool. You look inexperienced, which you are. Her trying to shine a spotlight on your flaws only makes *her* look foolish." Matthew put an arm around me and pulled me into him. "Don't let her win."

"I don't have much of a choice," I said and forced myself to laugh to downplay my frustration.

After a few minutes, Vladimir disarmed Mallory —though I bet he could have done it much sooner— sending her weapon skidding across the mat.

"Whenever you think you're at the top of your game, you'll find out you're not—there's always another level," Vladimir said to Mallory, then handed me back my sabre. "Continue."

I stalked back onto the mat and faced off with Mallory, who raised her sabre in preparation of our next match.

"Say when," she said.

But instead of providing a warning, I simply slashed at her, commencing the fight. I was still unable to throw her off, but at least I got a few more strikes this time. But to reassert her dominance, she moved beyond our fencing parries and surprised me with a martial arts attack. Mallory grabbed my sword arm, twisted me around, then grappled me to the mat. My head slammed into it hard with only one hand to catch my fall, the other—my injured hand—trapped behind my back.

My ears were ringing, but I still thought I heard a whistle being blown. I felt Mallory's bodyweight lift off me, then a faint word. "Dead."

"That's beyond the scope of this exercise," Vladimir said.

"Sorry; I got excited," Mallory said. "I needed

something to break the monotony with my inferior sparring partner."

My blood was boiling, and as soon as I could, I sprang to my feet and tackled Mallory from behind. I knew it went against everything Matthew had said. I knew she could best me at this too. But in that moment, I didn't care and proceeded with my attack anyway.

I was on top of Mallory for only a fraction of a second before she was able to flip me off her and reverse the tables. The next thing I knew, she had her strong legs wrapped around me, immobilizing my body, her arm snaking around my throat, fully ending my assault with a headlock.

"That's enough! Break it up! Break it up!" Vladimir yelled, yanking Mallory off me—lifting her off the ground entirely and dropping her a few feet away.

I pried my mask off, coughing violently as I lay on the mat. Matthew was now kneeling at my side, laying a soothing hand on my back.

"That was kind of the opposite of what I told you to do," he said. "Are you okay?"

"You all saw what she did," Aaron said angrily, now at Mallory's side. "She must be getting her temper from her coach. This can't be allowed to continue."

"You're right," Matthew said, his nostrils flaring.

"Something needs to be done about you—your entire family!"

Barry and Zelda had stopped sparring and were now watching us, along with quite a few other people throughout the gymnasium.

"You'll have to take it up with the Assembly," Vladimir said. "But the two of you are done with group training for this evening. Please leave the gymnasium."

"Gladly," I said, removing all my protective gear, and defiantly leading the way out of the training room. I stormed into the locker room and changed as quickly as possible, so I might be gone by the time Mallory got there, but she just couldn't leave me alone.

She strolled in a minute later, a scowl permanently etched on her face. She scoffed at the sight of me and headed straight for her locker. Amidst undressing, she said, "I hope you enjoyed your night with the freaks. You make a good toy for them."

I knew she was baiting me, so I held my tongue, trying not to get myself into more trouble.

"Oh, and by the way, I requested your termination from Hot Coffee. It's kind of a conflict of interest at this point. I thought you should hear it from me. Your friends won't be there for much longer, either."

"Are you serious?" I said, slamming the door of my locker. "You're unbelievable."

"With our reference, I'm sure they won't have any trouble finding work." Mallory smirked and wiggled into her slim jeans. "You, on the other hand, can join your mom cleaning houses—or whatever it is she does these days."

To be honest, I didn't know what my mom did for work anymore. She was typically juggling multiple jobs, with fulltime work being hard to come by. At one time she was a maid, but I didn't know how Mallory knew about that... unless she...

Oh... my... God... I couldn't have been more mortified.

Without saying another word, I rushed out of the locker room and slammed into Matthew as I flew through the door.

He caught my shoulders to stop me. "I was tempted to go in after you."

"Why can't you just kill her? It would make everything so much easier," I said, backing up a step to stand on my own.

"Trust me; it wouldn't."

MATTHEW

"*I*t seems we have a major problem," President Bolt said, seated at the far head of the oblong conference table.

The remainder of the Assembly of Seven filled up the rest of the conference table chairs. The other candidate coaches, Mac and Anderson, sat in chairs lining the wall, along with Octavius and Vladimir, while Aaron and I stood before the Assembly. The tension in the room was so thick, it made it hard to breathe.

"We have two candidates—legacy candidates—sabotaging each other at every turn," she continued.

"That's not entirely accurate," I said. "Fiona has endured the brunt of the abuse and remained steadfast and focused on her development."

"Those are not the accounts we've received," President Bolt responded. "I know you're both backing legacy candidates, and those candidacies are typically not much more than formalities. But that is not proving to be the case this time. There has become a major cause for concern."

"The accounts you've received are biased," I argued.

"As is yours," Douglas shot back.

Aaron tried to suppress a smirk as he stood at attention beside me, hands clasped behind his back.

"Matthew, you are the exception here and you've been given a great deal of latitude because you built this organization, but you have relinquished your rights as a voting member after the formation of the Assembly. That was before my time, but that is my understanding. Is my account accurate?"

"Yes," I said sadly.

"And with that, you must understand that the same exceptions and leniency does not therefore apply to your candidate." President Bolt leaned forward in her chair to appear as formidable as possible. "If these two cannot work together as candidates, how can we expect them to work together as members of the Society? We don't need more conflict and turmoil within our group, and right now there isn't a unanimous vote to admit either one of them. I don't care if they're able to pass the tests we've laid out for them tomorrow or six months from now—if they cannot be productive, reliable, trustworthy team players, then they're not going to be welcomed here."

"My daughter has exemplary skills and will be a great asset to the Society, especially with the rise of Vampire Nation," Douglas said confidently. "She's been primed for this her whole life."

"Obviously, not well enough, since a key aspect is working harmoniously within a team," President Bolt retorted. "You of all people should know her fighting skills are only part of the equation."

"This is not what we discussed."

"We discussed things further without your presence since it involves your daughter."

"The exact reason I should be present!"

"And a decision has been made for what they will be required to do, and if they agree, then there will be no going back," Ashley said. "It is something we've used in the past, so it isn't new. We've reserved the right to use this more immersive method of testing our candidates in years past, though not since this more conservative assembly has taken over."

Ashley had told me her plan, and as she'd expected, I wasn't keen on the idea for Fiona, though I'd supported it wholeheartedly in the past. And as expected, Douglas was livid since he was a major opponent of the practice, after being granted a seat on the Assembly—when Roland Damascus was voted to relinquish his seat.

"You better not be talking about reinstating

mandatory incarceration," Douglas said, glaring at Ashley.

"We talked about it and it's decided," Ashley said, glancing at President Bolt for support.

"And the girls will be roomed together," President Bolt added.

"I vehemently oppose my daughter being subjected to such torture!" Douglas yelled, his face growing beet red.

"This is the unanimous decision since I revoked your ability to vote for this motion."

"This is unacceptable!" Douglas slammed both fists on the conference table.

"This is the only way to move forward with these two candidates."

Aaron didn't look so confident anymore, his face haunted as he stared at the far wall.

"So, what's next," I chimed in, momentarily getting everyone's attention off Douglas's outburst.

"We'll arrange a time to bring Mallory and Fiona back to Singularity Room," President Bolt said. "I will meet with them personally to give them their choices."

"Very well," I said. "I will make sure Fiona's there at the requested time. Thank you."

Aaron glanced apprehensively at his father, who gave no indication of direction. Aaron finally took it upon himself to respond. "I'll get Mallory there as well."

"Then we have nothing more to discuss," President Bolt said, rising from her chair. "Do not prepare your candidates any more than you already have. I want to deliver the news of the next leg of their journey myself."

Douglas looked quite crestfallen, giving me a small sense of satisfaction. Mallory had been actively trying to get Fiona to quit since the beginning and now they were being punished together. It seemed Mallory had been given special treatment her entire life, so it was satisfying to learn that her father wouldn't get her off the hook this time.

Despite my pleasure in Douglas's loss, I still feared for Fiona—well, for both girls actually—and hoped they would ultimately become stronger for it, like in the case of Ashley Degray. But I'd seen the pendulum swing the other way too, with candidates coming out broken, never recovering to their former selves.

FIONA

I went with Alexis to our evening shift as usual, curious as to what would be waiting for me when I got there. I didn't mention my possible dismissal to Alexis or Candace while we were at school, not knowing how to explain it without diving into my new double life. And maybe Mallory had been bluffing.

My fears were realized when the store manager, Michael O'Brien, was still there that late in the afternoon and called me into the office while I was waiting for Candace to finish making my white mocha. He confirmed the seriousness of the situation when he asked me to close the door before sitting down.

"There's no easy way to say this, so I'm just going to say it," he began. "I have to let you go."

Since I'd been anticipating this discussion, I

didn't look particularly shocked, which surprised him. This had been my first job—so I had nothing to compare it to—but I'd really liked it, especially getting to work with my best friends. It would feel weird coming here and not jumping behind the counter and being able to make my own drinks. But I remained strong and didn't get emotional. Instead, I simply asked, "Are you going to tell me why? Did I do something wrong?"

"I'm sorry, but this is coming straight from the owner. He's requiring me to cut costs, and a big part of that is labor. We are going to start running leaner shifts. And with less hours in the overall pool, we'll have to do a few layoffs. Your name was specifically mentioned due to your limited availability."

"Alexis has the same availability as I do," I argued, which immediately made me feel guilty for dragging my friend into this.

"Which is why one of you was a good place to start the cuts. Alexis has more experience, is a model in exemplary customer service, and has reliable transportation." Michael picked up a sealed envelope from the desk and handed it to me.

"You're right," I said. "I don't want to insinuate I'm better than her because I know how awesome she is."

"I know you two are close." Michael pointed to the envelope now in my hand. "That's your final check. I'd appreciate you turning in your aprons when you can."

"Sure," I said, not willing to fight anymore. "Can I go now?"

Michael nodded.

I had the apron I was going to wear on shift that day folded at my waist, so untied it and tossed it to him. "I've got three or four more at home, but I'll bring them in."

As soon as I opened the door, Candace was standing there, holding my white mocha in one hand and reaching for the doorknob with the other. "Here you go," she said, not even suspecting anything was wrong.

Without her noticing, I stuffed the envelope into my back pocket and rejoined Alexis at the bar, still five minutes away from the start of our—her—shift.

"I'm so not looking forward to the history test tomorrow," she said. "I haven't had a chance to study at all. And since we're closing tonight, I've got like no time. And I can't pull an all-nighter again." The closed textbook was next to her on the counter, like it was going to give her encouragement to open it.

"I've only done a little reviewing," I said. The truth was, I now had all evening to study, if that was where I wanted to put my focus. The problem was, I really didn't. With everything I was preoccupied with lately, I didn't have the focus or the mental or emotional stamina to study.

"Well, you'll probably do better than me." Alexis gulped down the rest of her iced tea and hopped down from the bar stool. By the time she'd strolled around the bar, she had her apron up and over her head, headed for the register. "Aren't you gonna clock in?"

"I was let go," I said, then took another sip of my white mocha. I wanted to savor it, not knowing if this was the last free one I'd be receiving.

"No way!" Alexis gasped.

"Are you effing kidding me?" Candace shouted from the espresso bar. I hadn't realized I'd said it loud enough for her to hear. "On what grounds?"

"Cutbacks, according to Michael," I said. "But I have good reason to believe Mallory was behind it."

"I don't doubt it—that bitch," Candace said, rounding the pastry case, then glancing at an older woman ordering from Alexis. "Sorry… it slipped."

Alexis turned after handing the woman her change. "Do you want me to drive you home? I'm sure Michael can spare me for fifteen minutes."

"Naw; it's okay," I said. "I can walk." I had already planned on doing so anyway, not that I really wanted to go home. I didn't want to tell Mom I no longer had a job. The thought of finding a new one and having to subject myself to interviews again sucked. It was one more thing I didn't want to think about. Perhaps the True North Society would pay once I became a full-fledged member and I wouldn't have to find a new job. That was the best-case scenario, but I wasn't counting on it.

While I continued to sip my drink, I noticed someone snag the stool beside me.

"Hey, Fee," Sean said. "You on a break?" He laid an envelope on the counter. The words *not at this address* were scrawled large across the front of it.

"Indefinitely," I said.

"What's that supposed to mean?"

"I don't work here anymore."

"Is that a good thing or a bad thing?" he asked, turning on his stool to face me.

"I don't know. I haven't decided yet," I said and glanced down at the envelope.

"Oh, it's just another letter that came back the other day. I thought you'd want it… you know, to cross off your list." Sean pushed it toward me.

"You don't have to do that. We're not together anymore."

"It's important to you, so I want to make sure you get them."

"Thank you," I said, picking up the envelope and examining my writing. This one had gone out nearly two months ago, according to the original post office stamp. I thought of the letter inside; I would hand write them all, thinking typing them would be too impersonal. Each letter was on college-rule notebook paper and gave a short synopsis of my life, who I was looking for, and how I came upon that address in my search. I received a few calls and emails, which were always nice. But most simply returned the letters, many times with ripped envelopes taped back up. This one had been patched up in such a way.

"Do you want to sit outside and talk?" Sean asked, causing me to look up from the envelope.

I wanted to ask why, but simply said, "Sure."

I caught Alexis's gaze as I stepped down from my stool and followed Sean outside to the wire-mesh table by the glass. She wasn't shy about letting me know she thought we ought to get back together. I wasn't willing to put so much faith in us.

"Do you want me to get you a drink?" I asked, once we were seated outside. Perhaps, I was looking for a reason to get away already. I didn't even know.

"No; I'm good," Sean said, giving me a shy smile.

We sat there for a while, neither of us willing to initiate the conversation. Sean had proposed the idea, so I was waiting for him; I'd given enough throughout our time together. He sat there, picking at his nails. I was about to get out my phone when he finally spoke up.

"How have you been?" Sean asked. He didn't look up at me when he asked the question, like he was embarrassed to be talking with me. After a moment, he added, "I don't like the way we left things."

"Wounds don't heal if you keep picking at them," I said, gazing down at my still bandaged left hand.

My right still had a hint of the X I'd been branded with at the nightclub. "I don't like how things ended either, but they did, so I'm doing what I can to move on."

"Then you're doing better than me. I've missed you." Sean finally glanced up, but once our eyes met, he dropped them again. "I hated what you were doing to yourself. But I also hate not having you in my life."

"You can't have it both ways." I didn't want to deal with this right now. I had so many other things on my mind. To be honest, I hadn't even thought about him in weeks. I'd been so preoccupied with all the new monsters in the world, that the collapse of our high school relationship just seemed trivial.

"What are you going to do now?" Sean asked after another long pause.

"You mean for work?" I asked, and he nodded. "I don't know, but I'm not going to worry about it right now. Maybe I'll just take the rest of the school year off. Get through finals and graduation."

"Do you know where you're going next year yet?"

"I don't have all the responses back, but whatever I choose, I'll stay local." I couldn't leave Becca and had never told anyone about her ghost, not even Sean.

"I see. So, we'll be a continent apart."

"A fresh start."

"Yeah; I guess so," he said, sounding quite

emotional about the idea. We'd talked about going to the East Coast together, but I knew I was never going to follow through with it. I never intended to show my acceptance to Penn to anyone.

After another awkward silence, Sean asked, "How are you getting home? Do you want a ride?"

"I've got it covered," I said. "But thanks for the offer."

"Okay… well, I did what I came here to do. I should go." Sean rose from this chair and simply stood there for a minute, like he was waiting for me to stop him, but I had no intention of doing that. When he realized the conversation truly was over, he said goodbye and left for the parking lot, not even stopping inside to say anything to Alexis.

I remained at the table a while, finishing my white mocha and people watching. For all I knew, some of them weren't even people—or, not human, at least. I tried watching people I thought were weird or suspicious, but those were most likely the most human of us all. The supernatural creatures blended in with us—emulating the best of us. The most beautiful. The most refined. The most like what the rest of us regular people wanted to be.

When I got tired of trying to pick out the monsters from the crowd, I gazed down at the envelope that Sean had brought. I'd saved all the previous envelopes and letters like a roadmap of my journey. But now, I realized this journey was over and I didn't need them anymore. I knew where my father was. I just needed to get initiated into the True North Society and I'd be taken to him. As Matthew had cryptically told me on our first meeting—my search was over.

I crumpled up the envelope and tossed it in the nearest trash can as I began my trek home.

MATTHEW

I hadn't planned to go to an AA meeting that night, but the hunger was overwhelming, what with everything that had been going on. To me, meetings seemed to be what it must feel like for all the other AA members to have to sit in a crowded bar—temptation was all around, but the support was still helpful. I also needed to continually test my resolve, forcing me from the confines of my prison apartment. However, I spent the meeting standing in the back of the room by the refreshments, afraid of what I might accidentally do.

While the others shared their stories, I sipped on stale coffee. It sure wasn't the "best damn coffee in the county" like they had at Fiona's workplace, but it kept me occupied and my focus off drinking—well, other liquids.

I'd called Jezebel, my sponsor, to tell her I was

coming tonight, so she'd promised to make it too, though she'd be arriving late.

When she slipped into the sectioned multipurpose room of St. Paul's activity building, she spotted me by the tables and came over.

"Did you make it?" she asked upon reaching me. There were no donuts that night, so she grabbed a lemon poppy seed muffin and a napkin.

"I did," I said. "I'm still dry."

"I'm proud of you," she said, offering me a hug.

I reciprocated, but made it just fleeting and then took a few steps back—keeping my distance without making it look obvious.

"Ouch; you need to watch that strength," she said, cracking her shoulders. "You're a lot stronger than you look."

"Oh… sorry," I said. I hadn't even realized I'd been so careless. I needed to focus. My compulsions didn't control me—I controlled them. I poured myself another sour coffee.

All the stress revolving around Fiona and Mallory was making it so hard to think clearly. Maybe Ashley was right, and I shouldn't be depriving myself of my true nature to remain at my best—my optimal performance. I certainly wasn't at my best right now. However, I knew Ashley would not have made such a bold statement fifty years earlier. She'd been horrified by my true nature when I'd first met her, as were most humans. But there were those exceptions, who seemed to be growing in recent years—hence the expanding Vampire Nation —those willing to offer up their blood for pleasure, adventure, and asylum. Of course, they were always playing with fire since there was never a guarantee they wouldn't be killed in the process.

"Are you going to sit or stand back here by yourself for the entire meeting?" Jezebel asked.

"I'm not really in the mood for sitting," I said.

"We're all in this together. You don't have to isolate yourself. You're not alone."

"I understand that," I said. "And I'm here because of the support, which I'm more than grateful for. But I'd just rather stand. I'm too antsy to sit."

"Fair enough," she said. "Well, I'm gonna sit and I'll save you a seat in case you decide to join us."

As I continued to listen to stories from the other members, my phone buzzed in my pocket, so I fished it out and checked the screen.

It seems someone beat us to the punch, the text read.

I clicked to open the messages and found three pictures attached below the text from Jack.

Martin Harner. There's not much left of him.

The first picture had been taken from the back of a dining room chair, positioned in front of a sunlit window. Wooden spikes were driven into the chair arms. The second picture faced the front of the chair, where the spikes could be seen better. The seat itself had multiple burn marks. On the cushion and surrounding floor were piles of ash, but no blood—his blood would have turned to ash with the rest of him once the sun finally killed him. The third image was a closeup of a framed picture, with the man we'd seen in the video clearly identifiable.

It's possible this was his doing to someone else, but I doubt it. Continuing to investigate.

It would take an hour or two for direct sunlight to kill a vampire without sun serum or some other UV-reflecting agent. The more direct skin it touched, the faster it burned through our bodies. The chair had been brought to the window on purpose. The wooden stakes through his arms would have helped immobilize him. God knew what else had been done to him to keep him in that chair while the sun slowly cleansed him with fire.

This was the vampire who had caused Fiona's accident, and there was a very good chance he had been tortured and murdered. I was positive he'd been working for Frederick, but if that was true, then who wanted to retaliate besides myself? In truth, the events could be completely unrelated. With everything Frederick had his hands in, the retaliation could have been for something else entirely.

This didn't mean Fiona was safe—because if nothing else, I knew she never would be safe from Frederick—it just raised more questions.

Keep me posted, I texted back.

I took a deep breath and tried to bring my focus back to the meeting—to listening to the stories of everyone else's demons, the internal battles everyone in this room was committed to fighting day in and day out. It would be so much easier to just stop fighting and give in to what we all truly wanted, but that was why we focused on the battles and not the war; it was easy to lose perspective during the war—to lose focus.

This was how I proved I was not like the others. This was my penance for what I was and the terrible things I'd done over the decades. It wasn't like I could just kill myself and rid the world of one more bloodthirsty vampire. My mission wasn't complete yet. So, I would remain thirsty...

I didn't know if I could manage it forever—until next year, or even 'til next month. But I could at least manage it for one day. That was my battle. The next day would be a new one.

FIONA

*M*atthew picked me up for another training session on Friday evening, and this time I allowed him to meet me at my apartment. It helped that Mom was working tonight.

I couldn't seem to stop the flood of fear and longing as I climbed into the SUV next to him. His smile seemed forced, giving me the feeling he didn't want to see me. I smoothed out my bangs and bit my lip as I focused my attention forward. Luckily, it was already dark outside, and once we were driving, our more telling features were masked by shadows.

"Please, tell me we're doing something else tonight," I said once we exited my complex.

"No fencing tonight," he answered.

At first, I sighed in relief, but then began to wonder—obsess about what that really meant. I wanted to ask him what awaited me, but since he wasn't offering, I was afraid to find out. What could I be worse at than fencing? And then there was seeing Mallory again. The mere thought of her increased my blood pressure. My hands began to shake from sheer hatred.

We headed back to the headquarters building on the prison compound. I still didn't know how the True North Society seemingly had this level of government access, but it was obvious that they had connections and money. Someday I'd hopefully find out just how far their reach extended.

Every few minutes, I stole a glance at Matthew, but he never seemed to notice—or maybe he did and simply didn't want me to notice he was noticing. His face was so beautiful in the moonlight, glinting off his fair skin. I wanted to reach over and touch him, but like reaching out to touch a wild animal, I was afraid of getting bitten or worse.

When we reached the underground parking structure, he didn't pay me any more attention, simply got out of the vehicle and expected me to follow. His jaw was tight, and his brows furrowed like he was fuming about something. I didn't know if it was something I'd done and felt far too nervous to ask.

We took the elevator several floors up in silence, then went to a private office, which may have even been the same one I'd changed in before the candidate branding ceremony. I looked down at my left palm, at the bandage still covering it. I'd cleaned the scabbed cut that morning and replaced the bandages. The skin around it had been bright red and was still sore to the touch, but it was healing. Soon I would no longer need the bandage, and the line across my hand would be just another scar to add to the collection.

Matthew closed the door. The anguished and haunted look in his eyes was even more present now. I looked around for a new set of clothes for me to change into but didn't see any. "What are we doing here?" I asked, turning back to him.

"Have a seat," he said, pointing to the couch against the wall.

"Okay," I said suspiciously, yet did as I was told. "I'm seated; now what? I'm the one all freaked out about continuing training with Mallory around and paranoid of what everyone here thinks of me, but you seem in worse shape than me. What's going on?"

Matthew removed a capped syringe from his pants pocket. "I need to put you under again."

"What? No. I thought we were past this." The thought of being put to sleep again and having no idea where I'd wake up next was incredibly unnerving. "Please don't."

"It's not my decision," he said, removing the cap on the needle. "It's coming directly from President Bolt. It's the next step in your journey—that's all I can tell you right now."

"What's going to happen to me?"

"President Bolt will tell you everything. I won't let anything bad happen to you… I just need you to know that."

I noticed his hand shaking as he held the syringe at his side. I was already afraid, but his own fear was contagious. I couldn't image what would scare him —and didn't want to.

"I—I trust you," I said. I'd brought myself to say the words but wasn't sure if I truly believed them.

"Please try to remember that after President Bolt tells you what's coming next," he said, and before I even had a chance to respond, he crossed the room in a flash and stuck the needle into my neck.

Within seconds, I felt my body sinking into the couch… the room growing dark… and the cool lips of a vampire on my forehead as everything around me faded to blackness.

FIONA

I awoke on the glass floor with the brilliant image of the Earth below me, feeling like I was still in a dream. Maybe that's what this whole True North experience had been—a dream I couldn't seem to wake from. Maybe I never woke up from the car crash and was still lying in a hospital bed, trapped in this crazy alternate reality—some strange purgatory.

I didn't know which timeline option I preferred.

As I sat up, I found Mallory seated a few yards away, gazing out of the glass walls into deep space. I had remembered the view being convincing, but seeing it again, I couldn't think of a way that this was manufactured. It seemed so real—which brought my thoughts back to the purgatory possibility.

As the cloudiness of my head cleared, I realized there were two more people in the cylindrical glass room, but they were not the other two candidates. They were two women—one middle aged and the other a few decades her senior. They were both dressed in business slacks and buttoned-down blouses, both standing by the glass elevator, seemingly observing us.

"It seems you're both finally awake," the younger woman said, her voice sounding relatively familiar. She walked further into the open room and stood between Mallory and me. "I know you don't know me by face, but you probably recognize my voice. As a quick refresher, my name is Janice Bolt, the president of the True North Society and the United World Coalition. And this is my colleague, Assemblywoman Ashley Degray, an esteemed member of the Assembly of Seven, which is the governing council of the True North Society."

"Good evening, ladies," Ashley said.

I caught Mallory glancing at me while Janice was talking. For once, she didn't seem any more informed than I was, making her noticeably uneasy. But by the end of the introductions, Mallory had risen to her feet, doing her best to display the same power and confidence as she did in school. However, these were not women who were easily impressed or intimidated—that much was obvious.

"What's going on?" Mallory asked in her usual demanding tone.

"I have brought you here to discuss your options,"

Janice said. "It seems we have a problem with the two of you. And I am going to tell you how we resolve it and move forward."

"You don't understand—" Mallory started to say but was quickly cut off.

I thought it was best to remain quiet.

"I understand enough and we're not here to place blame and debate responsibility. You both are here because a problem was presented to the Assembly. It has become apparent that you two are having extreme difficulty working together. I don't think we've ever had candidates within the same class harboring this much animosity toward one another. Can you think of another example, Ashley?"

"No," Ashley said. "But we also do not have many candidates with preexisting relationships coming into the program. But we can't allow that to be an excuse."

"I want to share my deep disappointment with the both of you. I'll be honest, my initial judgment was to remove you from candidacy altogether. But both of you have very strong people backing you. The both of you are legacy candidates, so that is also taken into careful consideration."

"What do you mean by legacy candidate?" I asked, hoping it wasn't a completely stupid question.

"Someone with a family member who has gone through the candidacy program and been initiated into the Society," Janice clarified.

"I apologize for any lashing out I may have done," I said. "Mallory and I have had our differences over the years, but I should have remained focused on my training and not our rivalry." I glanced over at Mallory to see if she'd add anything.

"I apologize as well," she said, though the words rolled off her tongue like she was simply going through the motions. "I do not harbor any ill will toward Fiona and know I can do better going forward. Thank you for giving us this opportunity to continue on and learn from our mistakes."

"The decision will be yours if you wish to continue, but it will be something you'll have to confirm this evening before you leave. And once that decision is made, there will be no going back."

"I confirm," Mallory said. "I wish to continue."

I was about to say the same, when Janice interjected. "Not so fast. You will have the opportunity to continue, but not until you've completed an additional task—and it will be the hardest thing you've ever done in your lives. Ashley, please explain to our candidates what will be required of them if they wish to continue with the True North Society."

Ashley stepped forward. "How about the two of you standing next to each other? I don't want to have to keep looking back and forth."

Mallory took a few steps to the side, but made me come most of the way to her. She didn't visibly scowl at our proximity, but I could feel the resentment she radiated.

"That's better," Ashley said. "It's time you get used to each other's company and working together, otherwise it will be a long, ugly road for you both."

I didn't like the sound of that one bit, and the look on Mallory's face told me that she agreed—probably one of the first things we'd been united on.

"Now, to put your minds at ease slightly, other candidates have gone through a similar requirement, though it hasn't been done for quite some time," Ashley said. "The True North Society is associated with a special hospital—a vampire-run hospital with human patients. I won't get into all the nuances of the hospital here, but it is a unique training facility, mostly for new vampires, but on occasion it has been used for Society candidates."

"Are you talking about Sisters of Mercy Psychiatric Hospital?" I asked, remembering the business card Matthew had given me when we'd first met, which seemed so long ago now.

"I should have known Matthew would have said something," Ashley said, glancing over at Janice, who didn't look overly pleased.

"He didn't tell me anything about it," I said, trying to backtrack and hoping I hadn't gotten him in trouble. "He gave me a business card before I was even introduced to any of this."

"Well, I *am* talking about Sisters of Mercy,"

Ashley said, looking me directly in the eyes. "And if you want to continue your journey with the True North Society, then you will be voluntarily committing yourselves to the psychiatric hospital for however long we deem fit. You both will share a room and go through the experience together."

"What kind of... experience... are we talking about?" Mallory asked.

"I'm not going to lie to you—it will be rather unpleasant. You will be at the mercy of the hospital staff, to treat you and feed on you as they wish. All I can promise you is that you will not be killed or suffer permanent physical damage. It will be a traumatic physical and emotional experience that you will endure—together."

All color had drained from Mallory's face, and from the queasiness I was now feeling, I probably didn't look much better. This sounded like I was going back to the vampire club, but this time, no one would be coming to my aid. We would be thrown in as toys and food for the vampires as our punishment for disturbing the peace within our candidate class—all thanks to Mallory Fiennes. If I didn't have just cause to hate her before, I sure as hell did now. I knew that wasn't what I was supposed to be thinking—the type of vengeful thinking that landed me here in the first place.

"You can't do this," Mallory finally said. "The

vampires are the enemy. My father wouldn't allow it."

"Your father was not given a choice," Janice said, stepping up. "This decision was not made lightly but deemed necessary. You will remain committed to the facility until you can fully count on each other for support."

"What if that never happens?"

"Then you'll never be released. As I said earlier, if you commit to this path, then there's no going back. You will see what few people ever see and live to tell about it. If you succeed, then you'll be released and continue your journey with the Society. If you fail, then you will become a real patient and be committed for life."

"The human patients of that hospital are never released?" I asked, my throat now terribly dry—all the moisture left in my body turning into sweat.

"There have been a few instances," Janice said, glancing at Ashley. "But they are exceptionally rare."

"And if we refuse?" Mallory asked defiantly.

"You were so confident about continuing a few minutes ago. If you refuse, then the True North Society will become a distant dream for you. Your father and brother will be tasked with making sure you never speak about what you have seen to anyone, and you better believe they've made people disappear for the secrecy and security of our organization. So, the question becomes: how much do you really want this?"

It had all been hard, but I'd come so far, and didn't know if I could live with myself if I quit now. I'd been looking for my father for years, and now I'd found where he was, how could I quit just before meeting him? For all I knew, he could have been one of the cloaked figures in the ceremonies. Matthew had told me numerous times earlier on that I couldn't quit—he wouldn't allow it—but he hadn't said that this evening, which now struck me as strange.

"How is this going to work?" I asked. "Are we simply going to disappear for days, weeks—months? What do I tell my mother? We're graduating in a few months. If we miss more than a few weeks of school, then we might not graduate with the rest of our class."

"We will arrange for you to take your GEDs before committing yourselves to the hospital," Janice said. "And you will tell no one about the hospital or the time you will be away. It's a harsh thing to do to your families, but it's necessary. If you perform appropriately, then you will see them again soon enough."

"What about college?" Mallory asked. "I was all set to go to an ivy league school. Now just getting my GED will probably screw all that up.

"You're not understanding the reach of the True

North Society. Forget about what applications you've submitted. We have connections with the most prestigious schools in the country, as well as our own training and academic programs. Wherever you want to go, we can most likely get you in. But the truth is, you won't be graduating from college... there isn't enough time left."

38

FIONA

"What does that mean?" Mallory asked, posing the exact question that immediately ran through my head.

"This is where I must insist you provide me with an answer," Janice said, turning away from us and strolling toward the glass wall, looking out into space.

"It for all the world seems like we're on a space station," I said. "How is that possible?"

"I need your final answer, then everything else can follow." Janice kept her back to us and Ashley went to join her.

"We're just supposed to let the vampires take advantage of us until you say *enough*?" Mallory asked. "What's the point?"

"To get us to bond," I said.

"From torture?"

"Shared trauma."

"And so, you come to fully understand and appreciate what we're up against," Ashley said, turning back to face us. "You will also come to realize that vampires aren't that much different from us. They too have a spectrum. Their nature is predatory, not evil. Do we label the lion as evil for killing and eating the gazelle? Do we label ourselves as evil for killing and eating other animals? There are those who indulge in their nature, and those who fight it. You will not fully understand until you are submerged."

"And what do you know about it?" Mallory challenged. "Looking down from your ivory tower? We're going to be the ones locked and tortured in the dungeons."

"I was reborn in that dungeon!" Ashley's voice boomed throughout the room—much more commanding than I originally gave her credit for. "I have gone through what you will go through, and worse because my captivity wasn't monitored as yours will be. There are worse things than the staff, whom you will not be forced to endure! And guess what, I was your age when I was captured. Eighteen. So, I know everything about what you'll be going through. I'm the one who suggested the option to the Assembly, and that is the primary thing that's saved you."

"Saved us?" Mallory was as defiant as ever.

Ashley got right in Mallory's face—she stood several inches shorter, so had to crane her neck—but drew herself in as close as possible. "Saved you from allowing your petty teenage drama to ruin this extraordinary opportunity you've been given. But the choice is yours whether you're going to accept it. I will hand you the key, but I'll be damned if I'm going to put it in the lock and open the door."

"I accept," I said, which got everyone's attention. I thought of the nightclub and was petrified of what was coming next, but I trusted in the True North Society sufficiently to know they weren't leading me to slaughter. It was going to be difficult, but they weren't asking me to do something that couldn't be done—something beyond my capabilities. As afraid as I was, I had to trust that they were testing me, but at the same time really rooting for me to succeed. As they all stared at me, I reiterated my statement, fully projecting this time until my voice consumed the room. "I accept."

Janice left her place by the glass wall and approached me. "You are confirming to voluntarily commit yourself to Sisters of Mercy until we deem you are fit to continue your candidate training?"

"Yes," I said, a little less confidently this time—afraid, but still as committed.

She nodded, giving me a small smile, then turned to Mallory. "How about you? Are you going to be shown up by your friend?"

"She's *not* my friend," Mallory argued.

"Then you're quitting?"

There was a long pause. Mallory gave me an anxious and worried glance, then said, "No. I'll see it through."

"Then you accept?"

"Yes."

"And you understand the terms?"

Mallory swallowed hard. "Yes."

Janice stepped back to address both of us, with Ashley falling behind her. "I require your final answers right now. Do you accept?"

"Yes," Mallory and I said in relative unison.

"And you also realize that there is no going back from this point—no reconsiderations, no appeals, and no evasion? Verbally, confirm you understand."

"I do," we both said together again.

"Then your test date is set," Janice said. "And we'll see how committed you really are." Then she carefully sat down on the glass floor, which she had difficulty doing. "Please, join me." Once Mallory and I also lowered ourselves to the disconcerting floor, she continued. "I offhandedly mentioned earlier that there wouldn't be enough time for you to complete college. Your confirmations to the next step have earned you an answer—and the answer reveals the True North Society's biggest secret, and where we derived the name from. It is the reason we have been able to accomplish what we have. It is the reason you are here. And it is the reason we know that the world as you know it will end in three short years."

It felt like my heart stopped, yet couldn't be certain I had even heard her right. But again, it was Mallory who spoke up first.

"What did you just say?"

"Your ears did not deceive you. The world as you know it will end in three short years."

"How in the hell can you possibly know that?" Mallory argued. "No one can tell the future."

"No, but we can recall from history," Janice answered. "Look down at Earth. You're not seeing what you think you're seeing."

"It couldn't possibly be," I said. "We couldn't possibly be on a space station, not to mention journeying here and back within the same night."

"Rockets can get into space in the span of a few minutes, so the timeline you're thinking of is not the impossible part. But this *does* all revolve around timelines. Look down at Earth. That really is Earth and you really are on a space station. It is called ParallEarth—and this special room is called the Singularity Room—both of which are being built in the Nevada desert as we speak."

I didn't think my heart would ever restart. Now I was certain I was still trapped in a dream—in the hospital with Mom trying to reach my comatose mind from my bedside.

"What are you saying?" Mallory asked, appre-hensively.

"You are on ParallEarth, looking down at your home planet from the year 2117."

"What? You have a freaking time machine?"

"We have a time parallel portal," Janice clarified. "So, we know what's coming and have been preparing for it for decades."

"Then you can stop the end from happening," Mallory said, fully engaged now—if not a little panicked. "If you know what's going to happen and you've been preparing for it, then you can stop it."

"The future is not designed to be changed, but to come to fruition."

"So, what's going to happen?" I asked.

"Are you familiar with Vampire Nation yet?"

Mallory and I nodded.

"Good. Well, they will soon introduce themselves to the world, which will cause a large host of prob-lems. They will eventually try to take over and we will retaliate by releasing the fires of Hell upon them. Members of the True North Society, along with a selected few more, will be safely in space by the time the nukes are launched."

"Everything will be destroyed?" I asked.

"No; not everything. But the world as we know it now will be destroyed," Janice said. "We'll lose access to the ground when Armageddon comes."

"We'll have to spend the rest of our lives on a

space station—essentially *this* space station?" Mallory asked.

"Twenty-seven years." Janice's eyes looked haunted and she temporarily dropped her gaze. "After twenty-seven years in space, a new portal will open, which will lead us back to 1949, and thus, the cycle will begin again. I may be old and potentially gone by that time, but both of you are young enough where you'll have decades left to live, with the pleasure of enjoying a simpler time."

"Wait a minute," Mallory said. "So, if all this is true and the future can't be changed, then you already know we're going to get in, regardless of this new task of being committed to the hospital. And if we're included on the space station, then you also know exactly how long we're going to live."

"Both logical observations, but this is where the aspects of time travel get tricky. The portal is some kind of a universe anomaly. Some higher power fights to limit manipulation of the past from knowledge of the future. As such, when the portal opened, all our records on the station were lost in an instant. Written information disappears when brought through the portal. Electronic devices die when going through the portal. Due to these limitations, an abundance of specific information has been lost. Though we can recall a number of larger events, many smaller events and details have been forgotten throughout the years."

"So, you don't know if we make it into the True North Society or onto the space station," I said.

"No; our logs are incomplete," Janice said.

"How many of these portals are there?" Mallory asked.

"We've only ever found the one." Janice paused and glanced at Ashley. "Though we continue to look."

I walked past them, continuing all the way to the glass wall. I felt more like I was floating than walking at that point. It would have been a lot easier to dismiss these new revelations if the True North Society hadn't already rocked my world perspective with the existence of vampires and angels—tangible evidence of their existence in a world that believed them to be mythical creatures. I had very little reason to believe they were lying to me now—especially if they granted me one last request.

Gazing out at the brilliant Earth that was apparently not my own, I made my request. "Before committing myself to Sisters of Mercy, I'd like to see my father."

The room was quiet for a moment, so I turned to face the elder members of the True North Society.

"It would mean so much. And if anything should happen to me while I'm in there, then at least I would have gotten the chance to meet him once," I added.

The silence in the room was overwhelming as I

awaited an answer. Even Mallory seemed curious as to how Janice would respond. My years of searching were culminating in this one simple request, and it was ripping my stomach to shreds. My hands were combing through my bangs to hide the scar on my cheek before I even realized what I was doing. There was nothing the vampires in the hospital could do to me that would be worse than the waiting in that moment.

"I think that can be arranged," Janice finally said. And her few heartfelt words nearly brought me to my knees.

39

FIONA

hen Janice had been talking about a portal, I hadn't fully grasped what she was talking about. Upon reaching the Parall-Earth control room of Sector 7, we were brought to the one operational transport portal. There were eleven more that no longer functioned. At one time, each one apparently transported travelers to different compounds around the United States. The one mysterious portal now transported its travelers to the Southern California compound—just ninety-nine years in the past.

Ashley went through the portal first, followed by Mallory. I glanced back at Janice, who ushered me forward. I stepped into the metal cylinder, looking at the back wall that appeared for all the world to be solid. But that was where the hidden doorway was located, one that had remained open since 1949—

since the first travelers left the station and returned to Earth. I had watched Mallory disappear before my eyes by walking through the rear wall.

I stepped through and saw as a new world suddenly appeared. I landed inside a new metal cylinder, built to look identical to the one I'd left behind, but the room outside of it was new—long and narrow, like I'd entered a walk-in closet.

Janice was right behind and continued to push me forward. Built into one side of the wall were five-foot tall lockers. Janice briefly stopped and retrieved a handful of personal items. Once we exited the small corridor or closet, she closed a door, which completely disappeared into the exterior wall. A card reader and keypad were positioned in the middle of the section of wall where the door had just been.

Janice swiped her keycard and entered a code into the keypad, which caused a sliding door to the left to open. The room beyond was smaller, but similar to the control room we'd left in space. The room housed multiple wall screens, control stations, and one more metal cylinder.

"Does that lead to the station being built in Nevada?" Mallory asked, walking up to it and peering inside the dark cylinder.

"Yes; that's where it leads," Janice said. "Fiona, I want you to wait here. Mallory, come with Ashley and me."

Mallory and I locked eyes as she was led from the room, unsure of what to think about each other anymore. Our new shared fate was bound to profoundly change our relationship—but not even the True North Society seemed to know what the final outcome might be.

Janice didn't give me any further directions, so I sat in one of the control station chairs, making sure not to touch the glass keyboard or any of the expensive-looking computer equipment, which was sleeker and more elegant than anything I'd seen before.

The sliding door opened a few minutes later and Matthew and an older man I'd never seen before entered the room. I jumped up and held my breath for a moment, at first thinking Matthew had brought my father, but it quickly became apparent that the man looked nothing like the few pictures I had of my father, even having aged twenty years.

"So, I guess this is it," Matthew said. "What you've truly been waiting for. Just remember to manage your expectations. However you're expecting this reunion to go, it won't."

"I understand," I said. "I just need to see him—put all the wondering to rest. I'm not expecting some sappy Hallmark reunion."

The other man took a seat at the control station and began efficiently tapping away at the glass keyboard. "The chamber will be powered up momentarily," he said, without looking up from his work.

Matthew seemed to be keeping his distance as we waited for the chamber portal to be ready for us. He still looked distraught, which had concerned me earlier. I couldn't take my eyes off him as he stared at the far wall, at its many screens displaying random numbers for which I had no context. Soon after, he shook his head to escape his reverie and brought his attention back to me.

"I've got your purse stowed away," he said softly. "It's better to keep your stuff here."

"Okay," I said, wandering closer to him. "I assume you know I'll be visiting your psychiatric hospital."

"I'm aware, and fought to keep you out of there, but ultimately, the Assembly has the final say. I'm sorry I couldn't do more. I'm doing everything I can to protect you."

"It's okay, really. I trust you more than anyone else here."

"Which probably isn't saying much," Matthew said and finally cracked a smile.

I shrugged shyly but returned the smile. His smile had a way of making me melt, even in a situation as tense and anxious as this. A small dimple formed on his left cheek, but not his right. It was subtle, but one more beautiful characteristic that caught my eye.

"The chamber's ready when you are," the technician said, bringing us back to the real reason we were here.

"After you," Matthew said, extending a hand like a servant to royalty.

The cylindrical chamber was now alive with random lights and a low hum. Inside, the air was thick and electric, like we could be struck by lightning at any second.

Matthew closed the chamber door and took his position right beside me, the area inside just big enough for the two of us. My hand hung limp at my side, but as he inched closer, our hands brushed each other, creating a static shock.

"*Ouch*," I whined.

"Sparks are flying," Matthew said, straight faced as he repositioned himself to look at me.

I was about to laugh, but his hungry look forced me to bite my lower lip instead.

"Don't do that," he said. "It's… it's too much…"

"What? Bite my lip?"

A soft growl rumbled in the back of his throat. "Yes." His eyes refused to release me.

We were so close, I could feel his breath on my face—so close, I was almost afraid of receiving another shock. But even though he remained directly in front of me, he began to fade as the entire chamber filled with a white fog, starting at the floor, and rising to completely submerge us. The humming of the chamber grew louder and louder until every other sound was drowned out. Within seconds, I couldn't see anything around me or hear anything besides the roaring chamber.

As quickly as the chamber's activity had consumed us, it all dissipated, and Matthew was standing before me once again. Without saying a word, he slid open the door and we were now in the control room I remembered from the space station, much larger than the one we'd left, with twelve chambers lining the walls. All the oversized screens on the back wall were dark.

"Where are we?" I asked, scanning the room and finally seeing Sector 7 in large yellow letters.

"Nevada," Matthew said.

"I didn't think this kind of technology existed."

"It's exclusive to us. You should remember, we've been dissecting and recreating superior technology for the better half of a century. We had what you'd consider modern computers in an age when the most advanced devices took up entire rooms and could only perform rudimentary math equations."

"I guess it still hasn't sunk in that your professors were from the future," I said as we left the control room and navigated through the station.

It felt so much like when I'd walked through the space station with the president of the True North Society, except this time, instead of everything looking dingy and worn, it all appeared shiny and new. And when I passed by windows, instead of seeing brilliant stars and far-off planets, I now saw the inside of what looked like a gigantic airplane hangar.

"You said my father was involved with building this?" I asked as we continued down never-ending hallways.

"Yes; he was the chief designer, learning as much as he could about the station in space and bringing that knowledge home to build this one."

We passed a small number of people working on various aspects of the station, but for the most part, everything was quiet. There wasn't a lot of activity, like back at the headquarters building during the night.

After a long trek, we reached an open hatch and took a manlift elevator to reach the ground. As we crossed the remainder of the hangar, I glanced back at the massive station that might have been a mile long for all I knew. The station was suspended from the ground by scaffolding underneath and thick cables from above, looking like an intricate spiderweb of support.

"It's so huge," I gasped, in complete awe.

"This is only Sector 7," Matthew replied.

At the edge of the hangar was a bank of elevators, which we took—heading upward. Then we exited a small stand-alone building housing nothing more than the elevators. The night air was noticeably warmer than it was back home as we made our way across dirt terrain to reach a campus of rectangular buildings.

I felt like we were getting close, and with each new step, my anxiety grew exponentially. By the time we entered one of the buildings, I could hardly breathe—and on reaching the third floor, I couldn't calm the tremors attacking my entire body. Matthew hadn't taken me to some gravesite in the desert; we were approaching a room, which further confirmed that my father was alive, and I'd be speaking to him within moments.

And before I knew it, Matthew stopped at a closed door halfway down the hallway and removed his keycard. "Do you need a moment before I open the door?" he asked.

I couldn't believe the time had actually arrived. I had rehearsed in my head a million times what I'd say to him when we finally met, but now I couldn't think of a single thing. My mind went completely blank as my body continued to shake. As much as I thought I'd been preparing all these years, it had all amounted to nothing. I wasn't prepared for this at all; I'd never be prepared for this. But I couldn't simply hide in the hallway, either.

I shook my head since I was unable to form the words to speak.

Matthew pressed his key against the card reader, which flashed a green light, and a mechanism in the door clicked to signal it had unlocked.

I shouldn't have been surprised that the light was off when Matthew opened the door, though there was a nightlight providing the room with a ghostly orange glow. Matthew moved to turn on the overhead light, then thought better of it, and proceeded to light a nightstand lamp.

The room was sparsely furnished, the bed taking up a majority of the space. And there was my father, asleep beneath the covers, his back to the door.

Matthew stepped back to stand by the door while I ventured deeper into the room. Around the far side of the bed, a cushioned rocker was positioned close to the wall. I was afraid I was going to see something horrible as I rounded the bed to get a glimpse of my father's face. However, what I saw wasn't horrible, but familiar. I recalled the few pictures I had of him and recognized him immediately, though the features on his face were thinner, with deep lines and nearly white hair—but it was definitely him. However, he looked more than twenty years older. He didn't look middle-aged at all, as should have been the case, but like he'd been transformed into an old man.

I slowly sank into the rocker just as he began to stir. Feeling a presence or noticing the light, my father blinked his eyes a few times before fully opening them. Even in the dim light, I could see his blue eyes matched mine, both an amazing and irritating realization. When our eyes locked on one another, I didn't know what to do. I felt like a spotlight was on me and I was expected to do or say something profound, but I was suddenly dumbfounded. I couldn't breathe. My hands tightened into fists. I could see the growing recognition in his eyes as we gazed upon each other for the first time—and, as far as I knew, the first time ever.

"Look at how much you've grown," he said hoarsely, reaching forward and grabbing a pair of silver-rimmed glasses from the nightstand. "It's always a wonder how quickly time passes."

"You know who I am?" I asked.

He sat up and found the right positioning for the glasses on his nose. "Oh yes, I'd know that beautiful face anywhere, my dear child—Abigail."

My heart sank at the mention of the unfamiliar name. "My name is Fiona," I said. "I'm your daughter."

"No," he said, shaking his head. "I—I distinctly remember. I was going to take you to the moon. There's a station there. We were going to start a new life away from all these monsters. They look just like us. You don't know until you open them up. We were going to fly there until... you died. Then I couldn't bring myself to go alone. It had been your dream."

"I'm not dead; I'm right here," I said.

"Am I dead? Have you come to bring me home?"

He glanced around the room and settled his gaze on Matthew. "You're dead... I must be dead too."

"What's going on?" I asked, the shaking in my hands finally subsiding. "What's wrong with him?"

"To get as much information from the future station as possible, Roland literally spent years away from his own time," Matthew explained.

"I memorized everything!" my father exclaimed. "You can't take notes through the portal. They're wiped clean on the other side. Father time is a sneaky bastard."

"Written information is not the only thing that gets wiped or affected in passing through the portal. All electronic equipment is rendered useless."

"I never took off my watch. Look," he said and showed me his left wrist, and upon it a child's watch with a dinosaur on the face. "It hasn't worked for thirty years."

"He's gone through several watches over the years," Matthew said. "The biggest risk of time travel is spending too much time in an alternate timeline. The mind is slowly wiped as well."

"My mind is in perfect condition," my father protested. "I will be back to work in the morning. And I have an Assembly meeting in the afternoon. A full schedule. Kelly needs to type up my notes and have them to me by 7 a.m. So much to do; it's a wonder I can keep it all straight."

"Do you remember Susan?" I asked, trying to

bring his attention back to me. It was almost as if he'd already forgotten I was here.

"Susan? Of course, I remember Susan," he said, a smile spreading across his withered face. "She used to serve me at The Angry Goat. Such a beautiful young woman. She was probably not much older than you are now. I wonder whatever happened to her."

I had no idea what he was talking about. "Susan was a woman you dated. You got her pregnant before you disappeared. She had two girls—Fiona and Rebecca. Does any of this ring a bell?"

"It sounds familiar—like I read it in a book some years ago."

"No; it wasn't some story you read. It's real. Susan is my mother—and Becca's mother, before she died."

"You're dead," he said again. "I was so stricken with grief. Your mother's name was not Susan. It was… umm… Gillian. Yes; I remember now. I have a picture. It's right here. I'll show you." He opened the top drawer of the nightstand and pulled out a small picture frame. "Yes; there we are. This was such a beautiful day. We went to get ice cream. I remember it like it was yesterday."

He handed me the frame so I could recall what he thought I should remember… then I remembered the picture of the girl from his office. "This is Abigail?" I gazed upon the picture of the young girl, my father, and a woman—Gillian—whom I'd also seen before. I'd been to her house—on—on the day of my accident.

"Yes," he said. "Little Abby and your mother, Gillian. You died and Gillian moved away, leaving me all alone. But you've come back. You've come back." My father carefully stood and opened his arms. "I've missed you so much, Abby my dear. I love you so much."

Tears were beginning to sting my eyes as I gazed up at him, unsure of what to do. A part of me had yearned to hear those words my whole life. But I'd also spent many long and frustrating years furious with him for leaving—for disappearing. And here he was, confused and hurting, with no idea who I really was.

He took the picture frame from my hand and placed it down on the nightstand, then held his arms out again. "I don't know why you're here now, but I'm ready. I'm ready to go with you. Simply lead the way into the light."

I finally gave in, stood up, and folded into his outstretched arms. By the time he wrapped his skinny arms around me, the tears were falling in full force.

"You can't go with her tonight," Matthew said from the other side of the room. "Remember how much work you have to do tomorrow? The station needs you. The Assembly needs you."

"Of course. How could I forget?" My father kissed my forehead, then let me go. "I wish it was my time so I could go with you, but it's not. I still have much to do here. Everyone's counting on me."

"I understand," I said, sniffling and wiping my wet cheeks. "You have very important work to do."

"The *most* important," he reiterated. "But I'm sure we'll be together soon."

"Yes," I said, unable to say anything more.

"We should let you get back to sleep," Matthew said. "Big day tomorrow."

"The biggest." He got back into bed and pulled the covers up to his chin. "The biggest. Everyone's counting on me."

"And you won't disappoint them," I said, my voice cracking as I fought to get the words out.

40

MATTHEW

*I*t was heartbreaking to see Fiona's first interaction with her father. I wondered if I should have tried to prepare her for who she was going to meet, but the information given to her about the portal was too new. She still didn't understand enough of what was going on to really have time to process it. So, in the end, I allowed her to go in there unencumbered and let the interaction unfold naturally. Maybe that was a mistake. I didn't know.

Her cheeks were glossy as she rounded the bed and I turned off the nightstand light. I ushered her through the door and immediately found her in my arms as she wept with a careless abandon that she didn't allow herself to reach inside the room. Her body trembled against mine and I held her tight to try and give the support she needed.

"I just don't know what I'm supposed to feel," she said between powerful sobs.

"You don't have to force yourself to feel anything, just let it come naturally," I said, stroking her soft hair.

"I'm so angry and relieved and sad and confused... I thought I was prepared..."

"It's understandable to be feeling all those conflicting emotions. And, in time, you'll come to appreciate all of them." I brushed her cheek with my thumb, wiping at the tears, then kissed the top of her head.

She craned her neck to look up at me, her eyes still large and glistening. My lips hovered inches from her forehead, and without thinking, they met her warm skin. I felt her hands tighten around my waist as she continued to gaze up expectantly at me. Then without saying a word, she lifted onto her toes and pressed her lips to mine.

My hands moved up the contours of her body, finally settling on the sides of her neck, my thumbs gently massaging her jawline. Her lips were so soft and sweet, so intoxicating, that I only wanted more. More of her touch. More of her flavor. More of her...

By the time our lips parted, I could barely breathe. My heart was hammering away in my chest, and I felt hers was too as we remained euphorically intertwined. I simply couldn't let her go. My desire to protect her was too great—and I didn't know how I was going to do that while she was locked away in Sisters of Mercy. The thought of her in there could very well drive me mad.

"I'm sorry," she said after a breathless moment. "That probably wasn't appropriate."

"Don't apologize," I said, my voice only slightly above a whisper. I was afraid of my feelings toward this new development but didn't want to sound dismissive.

She apprehensively backed away, breaking eye contact as her focus turned to her fidgeting hands. "Don't hate me," she finally said.

"I could never hate you." I placed a finger under her chin and guided it upward, her sparkling blue eyes finding mine once again. And I couldn't decide on a better way to show what I thought about her than to offer another kiss, so I took her face in my hands and consumed her lips with a hungry fervor. Within seconds, her mouth opened and her tongue found mine, quickly reaching a sweet and sensual rhythm.

I hadn't even realized I was pushing her backward until she hit the wall. It took very little effort to hold her there with my body, reminding me of just how fragile she was. I felt my hunger taking over and actively had to force myself to pull back. The temptation was too great to tear into her—then I'd just be another one of those monsters in her eyes.

When I felt my fangs beginning to protrude past my other teeth, I quickly broke our union and stepped away.

Fiona's expectant and sorrowful eyes were fixed on me, her chest heaving, her lips swollen and red. "Don't do that if you don't mean it," she said.

"What makes you think I don't mean it?" I asked, bringing a hand to my lips, feeling the tips of my fangs in relation to the neighboring teeth. I seemed to have held them back, which was a small comfort.

"I don't know," she said as a sly grin grew on her tear-stricken face. "I just want to make sure I'm managing my expectations."

"That's very wise," I said, matching her growing smile.

We were just about to start heading back to the elevators, when Fiona grabbed my arm. "Can I request one more favor?"

I couldn't imagine what else she'd want right now, and I needed to get back home, so I could satiate my hunger before it became unbearable.

I will not give into my need tonight, I reminded myself. *One day at a time.*

"Of course," I said, my voice unsteady. "Name it and I'll do what I can to make it happen."

41

FIONA

I stepped out of the Land Rover after asking Matthew to wait inside. It felt so strange to be back at this house. There'd never been a reason for me to return to an address I'd crossed off my list. This was the first—1302 Wheeler.

The chalk drawings on the steep driveway were gone, washed away without a trace. The yellow compass held meaning for me now, even though it probably didn't for its young artist. Now I was curious what the context had been.

As I marched up the vertical driveway, I remembered Gillian's long red nails and realized I hadn't thought about them since the day I'd visited. Hopefully, they wouldn't strike the same raw nerve as before.

I removed the photograph from my back pocket

and rang the doorbell. I was nervous, but it didn't really matter what she said this time. I didn't blame her for claiming not to know my father previously, sure that he was a sore subject, just as he was in our household. But now I knew the truth—and I still firmly believed that knowing was better than wondering.

When Gillian opened the door, there was a moment of curiosity, then doubt, then recognition—quickly followed by irritation.

"What are you doing back here?" she asked sourly. "I thought I made myself clear—"

I handed her the photograph before saying a word—the one with her, Abigail, and my father.

"I told you I didn't recognize..." But then the people in the picture registered and she was momentarily rendered speechless. However, when her voice returned, it was in full force. "A teenage girl comes looking for my husband. What am I supposed to do with that? I assume you think he's your long-lost father. Well, he was a father to our daughter for a number of years—that is, until he upped and left without so much as a goodbye. We've been through enough and don't need someone new coming to tear our lives apart even more. We'd just like to move on in peace."

"I'm not here to tear your life apart," I said. "I'm not here to villainize him. I'm here to calm your doubts and offer the closure it's taken me years to find—probably a lot longer than he's been gone from your lives."

I noticed the long red nails against the door jamb and tried not to flinch, but they weren't rapping against the wood this time. They were still. Gillian was still, her attention fixated on me.

"I'm listening," she said.

"I didn't find Roland Damascus because there's nothing left to find, but I found out about him. He died in October 2015. I discovered that his body has since been cremated, so there's no burial site."

"That was the month he disappeared," Gillian said, her green eyes clearly haunted by a memory.

"He didn't abandon you and your daughter. He wanted nothing more than to remain with his family; I'm sure of it."

She eyed me skeptically, but something was hitting home. A tear spilled from one eye, which she quickly wiped away as she turned toward the inside of the house to obscure my view.

"He's dead?" she asked as she turned back to me. "Why have I not been told this by anyone official? If he was identified, then they would have notified his family—his wife of thirteen years."

"Because—because his death isn't official. It's not officially reported. He's just gone and there's nothing any of us can do about it. But the important thing is he didn't abandon you and your daughter.

He's not off starting a new family, leaving you behind. He's gone."

"Is that what you believe he did to you?"

"He never really belonged to my family, but he *is* my father. I had a twin sister, but she's gone too."

"Okay; this is getting to be a little too much. I'd appreciate it if you didn't come back."

"Who is it, Mom?" a young girl asked, entering the foyer from another room. Her hair was lighter than mine, but I could see similarities in her facial features. However, her glistening emerald eyes were all her mother's. She looked somewhere between ten and twelve.

"No one, honey. This girl was just leaving," Gillian said.

"Abigail? I'm Fiona," I said.

As Gillian began to shut the door in my face, I slammed my hand against it to prop it open.

"I know about your father," I continued, trying to get the words out swiftly—before my opportunity was gone for good. "I'm your half-sister."

"What? You do—you are?" Abigail gasped.

"How dare you!" Gillian hissed and pushed harder against the door. "Stop harassing my family!"

I finally stopped fighting and let the door slam shut. An argument ensued from inside, but the door didn't reopen. Footsteps stomping away were audible, alongside the slamming of another door.

"I'm sorry," I said, more to myself than anyone

else, then released the picture of their family from years past and let it float to the ground.

Once all was quiet inside the house, I headed back to the Land Rover and hopped inside.

"From what I can tell, that didn't go well," Matthew said, placing a soothing hand on my thigh.

"It could have gone worse," I said. "I don't exactly know how, but I'm sure it could have. But it's better they know."

"Not everyone will share that opinion," he said as we began our drive home.

"Just because they don't believe it doesn't make it any less true," I said.

"And I suppose you know what's best for everyone." Matthew laughed and slapped my thigh before returning both hands to the steering wheel.

"I have my opinions."

"You've made that abundantly clear. Is there anything else I—your humble servant—can do for you, Your Highness?" he asked sarcastically.

"I could use an Oreo right about now," I said—which was anything but sarcastic.

EPILOGUE: MATTHEW

My feelings for Fiona frightened me. She was already on Frederick's radar. The fact that this Martin Harner had most likely been eliminated was irrelevant. Even though I was sure Frederick was really behind the accident, we still couldn't trace Martin back to Frederick, nor did we know who'd killed him. Jack had told me he'd uncovered a lead and would hopefully be updating me soon.

I paced my prison apartment with a glass of warm wolf's blood, waiting for the sun to go down, so I didn't have to waste another dose of Sun Serum. Even with my connections, it was often in short supply with more vampires seeking its sanctuary. The sun was on the descent and would be sinking into the Pacific within the hour.

What the hell am I doing?

I knew better than to get involved with Fiona. I'd been watching her for years, waiting for her to come of age, so she could pledge the Society. I couldn't lose sight of the role she needed to play when the end came. By getting romantically involved with her, I was complicating the whole situation and putting her in more danger, when I needed to be protecting her.

But there was something about her that called to me—now that she wasn't just some target from afar—something primal and sweet I couldn't deny. And now the thirst, the hunger, the need had dug its claws deeper into me than ever before. The only way to keep from complete self-destruction was to abstain. I couldn't continue this way; I had to distance myself from her. She deserved better than me anyway for her final few years on Earth—yes, for her final few years—because I knew she wasn't going to make it onto ParallEarth with the others. She'd already be dead.

I shook the thought away with another sip of blood, gazing out at the world through the UV reflecting glass.

Even though I was terrified for Fiona to enter the darkness of Sisters of Mercy, it could actually work to my advantage. It might be better not to have the staff go easy on her. Her time in confinement with the monsters she feared could provide the perfect aversion therapy to drive the much-needed wedge between us. But then I thought about Ashley and Jack, the beginning of their story, and the love they'd shared for decades.

They're the exception, I told myself. *I'm destined to be alone.*

A buzzing interrupted my thoughts, and I crossed the room to grab my phone from the kitchen counter.

"Jack, what do you have for me?" I asked, placing my empty glass of blood in the sink.

"Something interesting," he said, his voice sounding hopeful. "It may be nothing, but then again, it may be..."

"Well, out with it, man. Don't keep me in suspense."

"I just emailed you a video. Check it out on your computer; the quality's rather poor."

"Fine," I sighed and booted up my laptop. I didn't fill the silence with small talk as I went into my email and clicked the attached video. "What am I looking at?" I asked as it began to play.

The video was grainy and lacked sound. It was obviously a surveillance camera feed, pointing out from a doorway. A busy street and building across the way were visible.

"The far building you see is Martin's apartment building," Jack said. "Do you see a woman exiting the building?"

"Yes," I said. "She's jogging across the street now."

"Watch her."

I did, hoping she would come into focus as she came closer to the camera. By the time she reached the sidewalk, I thought she looked familiar. Then when she turned and walked right past the camera, I was fairly certain I recognized her, even with the pixelation.

"Is that Susan Winter?" I asked.

"Yes."

I got a good glimpse of her before she strode off screen with obvious purpose. Her slender form, elegant gait, and long chestnut hair reminded me so much of Fiona. In this poor-quality video, someone who didn't know better could have easily mistaken one for the other.

"What's the timestamp on this video?"

"One day before we found Martin—or at least his apartment. We've had eyes on the building since then, as well as bugging his residence. There's been no other activity so far."

"Where is this apartment?"

"Diamond Bar," Jack said. "Over a half hour from where Fiona and her mother live. That was one of the big things sparking my curiosity. What was Susan doing there? Like I said, it may be nothing."

"Or it may not," I said and played the video again.

AFTER THE FINAL WORD

APRIL 5, 2019

I first and foremost want to thank you for taking a chance on a new series and reading *Angeles Vampire*, and now you're even continuing with the author's note! I'm so grateful and could obviously not do this without you.

This is a very unique series for me with a lot of backstory. The first ideas for the story came to me in 2013. In the beginning, the story was purely sci-fi / dystopian. There were no vampires, angels, or any supernatural elements. It all started with a space station and a time portal. The secret society was originally called the Aurora Alliance (also the original title) and there was going to be more schooling involved. It may have even turned into an academy book, well ahead of the explosion that's happening right now in the indie marketplace.

I wrote some notes and a few chapters, then put

it away to finish my *Higher Realms* series (at that time, called the *Lorne Family Vault*). When I picked it up again in early 2016, I added the vampire element, but not within the Aurora Alliance (which it was still called). Fiona was training with Aaron and he was to become the love interest. I wrote nearly a third of the story, under the title *Urban Vampire*. But then I stopped again, feeling there was something missing.

Once I finished the *Royal Replicas* series, I re-read the chapters and developed new ideas. Matthew had already been a background character in those previous chapters, but I brought him to the forefront, along with his rivalry with Frederick. Then the true *Angeles Vampire* was born.

However, when I originally released *Angeles Vampire*, I did it under a pen name. You might have seen the name Sofia Raine floating around in the internet universe. Well, that was me.

After some of the reader backlash I received from *Royal Replicas*, I talked with a marketing consultant and a few other authors, who all came to the general conclusion that a YA PNR series might be better received with a female author name. I'd never seriously considered a pen name before, but I wanted to give the new series its best chance for success, so I gave it a shot.

I created a new website, new social media profiles, a new Amazon author page, and released this book under the Sofia Raine name. And what I soon discovered was the author name really didn't do a damn thing.

Was it a mistake? Was I not giving readers enough credit? I don't know. It wasn't a success, that's for sure. The release of this book was met with crickets while the entire *Royal Replicas* series continued to sell without me pushing it at all (and even with the backlash). Even though the lackluster reception of *Angeles Vampire* was disappointing at the time, in the long run, it was a blessing in disguise.

One of the great things with indie publishing is the opportunity to adjust. I released the first few books in rapid succession, and by the time I was ready to release the third book and saw that this wasn't working, I pivoted. I pushed out the release of the fourth book, changed everything back to my name, and asked readers to forgive me for disappearing for nine months.

It was an experiment that ultimately failed, but one I needed to try. I would have always wondered if I hadn't taken the chance. What if? It's important to take chances in life. Sometimes I think I don't take enough of them. I don't mean simply being reckless —but taking calculated risks. Rewards come from taking risks, not playing it safe. And I want to continue to write and work toward those rewards.

I would love to keep Fiona and Matthew's story going, and for that, I need *your* help. If you enjoyed the book, then please leave a review, and tell your friends and the strangers standing in line with you at Starbucks (or Hot Coffee). Reviews and word of mouth are the best ways to support authors you love.

Thank you again, and I look forward to seeing you in the next story.

Onward,
Michael Pierce

FREE BONUS SHORT STORY!

How would you like to continue your journey into the *Angeles Vampire* world with an exclusive short story?

Sisters of Mercy continues the immersive experience and provides insider information from a new perspective. You can't get this *Angeles Vampire* short story anywhere else, and it's a must read for true fans.

If you're not already a member of my newsletter, then you'll also be the first to hear about my new releases, promotions, giveaways, and other fun stuff intended to lift your spirits.

What are you waiting for? Your exclusive *Angeles Vampire* short story awaits…

https://www.michaelpierceauthor.com//angeles-vampire-free-prequel

READ MORE BY MICHAEL PIERCE

THE ANGELES VAMPIRE SERIES (*Complete*)

Angeles Vampire Box Set

Angeles Vampire (Book 1)

Angeles Underground (Book 2)

Angeles Betrayal (Book 3)

Angeles Covenant (Book 4)

Angeles Prophecy (Book 5)

Angeles Reckoning (Book 6)

THE SPELLCREST ACADEMY SERIES

Spellcrest Academy (Book 1)

Crestfallen (Book 2)

Crystallize (Book 3)

Medial Candidate (Book 4)

Catacombs (Book 5)

Chrysalis (Book 6)

Sapient Curse (Book 7) - Pre-Order Now!

THE ROYAL REPLICAS SERIES (*Complete*)

Royal Replicas Box Set

Royal Replicas (Book 1)

Royal Captives (Book 2)

Royal Threat (Book 3)

Royal Return (Book 4)

THE HIGHER REALMS SERIES (*Complete*)

Provex City Box Set

Provex City (Book 1)

SUSY Asylum (Book 2)

Doria Falls (Book 3)

Archanum Manor (Book 4)

ABOUT THE AUTHOR

Michael Pierce is a young adult author of urban fantasy, paranormal romance, and sci-fi dystopian. His books are thrilling and unexpected, romantic and fantastical—addictive tales sure to keep you reading long past the witching hour.

Michael currently lives in Southern California with his wife, two children, and attention-craving chiweenie.

Connect with him online:
michaelpierceauthor.com
michael@michaelpierceauthor.com

Made in United States
North Haven, CT
29 March 2022